DAMNED TO HELL

DAMNED TO HELL

TRIALS AND TRIBULATIONS BOOK 2

NATALIE GREY
MICHAEL ANDERLE

DISRUPTIVE IMAGINATION

DAMNED TO HELL TEAM

Team Includes

Beta Readers

Dorene Johnson (US Navy (Ret) & DD)
Diane Velasquez (Chinchilla Lady & DD)

JIT Beta Readers - From both of us, our deepest gratitude!

Alex Wilson
Kimberly Boyer
Joshua Ahles
John Findlay
Micky Cocker
Keith Verret
Tim Cox
Ginger Sparkman
James Caplan
John Raisor

*If I missed anyone, **please** let us know!*

Editor
Lynne Stiegler

From Natalie

For M and T

From Michael

To Family, Friends and
Those Who Love
To Read.
May We All Enjoy Grace
To Live The Life We Are
Called.

Montpellier, France

A loud bang echoed, and the truck skidded across the center line toward oncoming traffic. Maurice Vannier swore and fought the steering wheel as cars hurtling toward him laid on their horns and swerved out of his way.

"I know! I know, goddammit!" he yelled back at them while turning desperately.

Did they not see the truck swerving? Did they think he was doing this on purpose?

Maurice gripped the steering wheel harder as it tried to jerk from his control. The road wound down the mountainside, and a steep drop-off lay only a few yards away. His mouth was dry with fear, even as his body went through the motions to pull the truck back across the lanes of traffic and onto the shoulder. Another few cars honked as they went past, furious at having been briefly inconvenienced.

Mercifully, he finally brought the truck to a stop and sagged back in his seat, heart pounding.

It was several long moments before he could convince himself to climb out.

He was still trembling, and he knew what he was going to see. He swore quietly to himself as he jumped down onto the shoulder and looked at the tires. One of the back tires was completely gone. Shreds of rubber were visible on the road behind him.

At least the rim wasn't bent.

But he wasn't going to get this cargo to Madrid on time. Not even *close*! The truck couldn't make it without the tires, and the Lord only knew how long it was going to take to get a replacement this far out.

"*Putain!*" Maurice kicked at the tire furiously. "*Va te faire foutre!*" He needed this job. Work had dried up. Anisa was threatening to leave him again. His landlord was always coming after him for the rent, which was always a week late at least.

He'd called in every favor he was owed, and had still had to wheedle Henri into giving him this job. The man had given him a lecture on reliability while Maurice'd bitten his tongue. He'd debased himself by listening, and now Henri was going to say giving him the job had been a mistake. And it wasn't his *fault*. It wasn't! A blown tire could happen to anyone.

But it happened to him. Of *course* it happened to him—and, of course it happened with the biggest payday their firm had seen in years. A big shipment to Spain; some rich person who didn't want too many questions asked.

If the authorities come, you do whatever you have to do to keep them from looking in the truck.

And of *course* they would come now, because the truck

was stuck in a mountain pass. Maurice pounded his fist on the side of the vehicle. Then, because there was nothing else he could do, he pulled his phone out and dialed Henri's number.

"*C'est moi.*" His shoulders slumped. "*Y a un probleme...*"

QBBS *Meredith Reynolds*

"And it's definitely stopped?" Bethany Anne leaned back in her chair and narrowed her eyes at the screen.

Yes, TOM confirmed. **ADAM was able to find satellite footage.**

"And..."

Yes. And it looks like there may be police inbound.

"Those shitbrained trailer-park-reject sonsa... You know what, TOM? This is what I get for trusting the French."

Why are there so many references to people hating France?

"Where there's smoke, there's fire, TOM. And this?" Bethany Anne narrowed her eyes. "Blown tire my *ass*. Someone's up to something." She pushed herself up and strode out of the room.

Where are you going?

"To find Bobcat. I'm getting a fucking airlift if that's what it takes, and then? I am reaming those fuckers out for this little trick."

She walked down the hallway, her voice reverberating off of the walls, "No one gets away with stealing my shoes."

Catalonia, Spain

The private plane bounced as the wheels touched down, jolting Jennifer out of her daze.

She sat up and straightened the borrowed coat reflexively. She liked to look good, and it had been a constant source of annoyance on the flight that not only was her nice jacket gone, she was wearing a lab coat that didn't even fit. She sighed. She was only focusing on the lab coat to keep herself from thinking about the mess she'd gotten into.

Her split-second decision to try to impersonate a scientist had landed her here, on Hugo Marcari's private jet. It was clear that neither Hugo nor Gerard trusted her, but they hadn't shot her yet—and she was fairly sure they didn't know she was a Wechselbalg.

Not only that, her link with ADAM was going to make it easy for the rest of the team to track her to Hugo's headquarters. It had been a good decision, she told herself.

But she was also pretty sure Stephen was going to be furious with her when she got back.

If she got back.

No. She wasn't going to think like that. Jennifer straightened her shoulders and settled back in the seat. She consciously kept herself from looking over her shoulder to see if Gerard was watching her. She'd caught him looking periodically through the flight. He made the hair on the back of her neck stand up.

She knew she could destroy him in a straight fight, but they were in a plane with two bodyguards, a broken Wechselbalg, and three guns that probably had silver bullets. It would be very, very far from being a straight fight.

She needed to make a plan.

Jennifer looked out the window as the plane rolled to a stop. The runway appeared to be in the middle of nowhere, surrounded by mountains covered in greenery. The blue sky above had only a few wisps of cloud.

"ADAM." She subvocalized as quietly as she could, aware of the chained Wechselbalg only a couple of yards away. "Where am I?"

>>**Catalonia, Spain. Hugo Marcari's family is from here. Since he owns many properties, your presence will help us determine which one to focus on.**<<

"Good." Jennifer hesitated. "And, uh...how's Stephen doing?"

>>**He has made it clear that he was not pleased that I told you I could help with your plan. Other than that, I am not certain.**<<

"Where is he?"

>>The team is on their way back to the *Meredith Reynolds*, with the exception of Stoyan, Irina, and Arisha. They stayed to take care of the Wechselbalg that were rescued in Velingrad. They're on the *ArchAngel* receiving medical treatment. Most of them are expected to make a full recovery.<<

"Most?" Jennifer swallowed hard. She knew Stephen hadn't wanted her to see the inside of the facilities, and in a way she regretted having gone. The memories of what she had seen were burned into her, and she knew that no matter how long she lived, she was never going to forget the battered bodies or hopeless eyes of the Wechselbalg in Velingrad.

Her eyes flittered out the window. She was afraid of what she would see in Hugo's stronghold.

>>Some of the prisoners appear to be suffering from psychosomatic issues. Although their injuries are healing, their distress is making it difficult for them to recover.<<

Jennifer looked down. At times like these she remembered what ADAM was—not a human who could feel pain or despair but an artificial mind that was still learning about the world. ADAM's clinical view of the prisoners was chilling.

>>Jennifer, did I say something wrong?<<

She had to try to explain it. Otherwise, how would he learn? But she didn't know how to approach this, and the plane was coming to a stop. She looked around as one of the bodyguards came to haul her up. "I can't talk right now."

That was all she could risk saying, for fear that the bodyguard would wonder why her lips were moving. She let herself be pushed roughly along the aisle and into the sunlight.

Gerard escorted Hsu after Jennifer. One hand squeezed Hsu's upper arm; she remained in handcuffs. When they reached the bottom of the stairs, he shoved her so hard that she stumbled as she reached Jennifer.

Hsu clenched her hands to keep from crying out and tried to keep her face emotionless. She recited her cover story to herself over and over in her mind: *I want to be here. I want to finish my work for Hugo. I am loyal to him. I didn't run away from Sofia. I am eager to prove myself.*

Such a person wouldn't fear Hugo or Gerard, because they would be sure their loyalty and good work would be rewarded.

With that in mind, Hsu kept her head up and a look of clinical interest on her face as Sergio, the captive Wechselbalg, was forced out of the plane to kneel on the tarmac.

She knew instinctively that Sergio was important. There had been countless Wechselbalg, both broken and unbroken, in the Velingrad facility, but Hugo's interest was captured by this one. Something about this man, with his bruises and not-quite-broken eyes, had gotten under Hugo's skin.

Some had broken slowly but surely and others had rebelled enough that Hugo's scientists had killed them, but this one had remained defiant. When he was forced to action, the way he capitulated somehow stole any sense of victory Hugo may have felt.

That was the leverage Hsu must exploit if her time with

Hugo did not end soon. Hugo Marcari thought of himself as careful and methodical and he believed he was a master strategist, but he couldn't stand it when things didn't go his way. When people did not treat him as the demigod he imagined himself to be. The more Hsu thought about it, the more she realized she wanted to break Hugo like he had broken everyone else.

It would not be enough for his experiments to end and the prisoners freed. She wanted him beaten down and stripped of every bit of power he had acquired, and before he died, she wanted him to know that he had failed *completely*.

She looked at 'Irina,' the other woman from the helicopter. Their eyes met for a moment before the scientist was hauled away, but Hsu thought she saw the smallest nod. She could only pray that meant there were allies on the way.

"So." Hugo settled back in his chair. He let his gaze drift over the woman in front of him. He wasn't stupid. When an absolute knockout miraculously escaped the carnage at Velingrad and managed to jump onto his helicopter, he knew enough to be suspicious.

He waited, letting the tension stretch; letting her get nervous.

People were infinitely more pliable when nervous. Gerard usually helped with that, but he was busy interrogating the survivor of the Sofia massacre, another woman. It occurred to Hugo that perhaps the women he hired were simply cleverer than the men—better at hiding and less likely to confront the prisoners if something went wrong. Perhaps they were better able to elicit sympathy, or perhaps, it was nothing more than coincidence. Only two scientists had survived the destruction of his facilities, and it could easily be a fluke that they were both female.

Or they could both be traitors.

Hugo's jaw clenched. This woman did not appear to be uncomfortable with the silence. She waited patiently for him to speak, hands folded in front of her and her eyes downcast. *What was she thinking?*

"So, Dr. Yordan…" He made his voice as harsh as he could. *"Hablas Espanol?"*

"Si, señor." Her voice was soft and she continued in Spanish, somewhat hesitantly. "I speak a little bit."

"And you understand me?"

"Si, señor ." Jennifer tried to keep her expression neutral. In truth, the man's accent was difficult to understand. "I…think so."

>>He's speaking Catalan.<< ADAM informed her. **>>It is more believable for you to speak a standard dialect, so I will not update your implant.<<**

Thank you, ADAM. Jennifer knew ADAM couldn't hear her thoughts, but she didn't dare move her mouth with Hugo watching her like a hawk.

"Tell me about your research," he ordered abruptly.

ADAM, help.

Luckily, ADAM was still listening. **>>Tell him you studied wolf pack structure and behavior, and you're here to achieve compliance in the prisoners. He's having**

**trouble maintaining control when they're in wolf form.
<<**

"I was brought here to help with the test subjects' behavior in wolf form." Jennifer swallowed her bitterness. "My specialty is wolf behavior and pack structure. Administrator Fedotov told me that there has been difficulty enforcing control after the subjects had shifted form." A surge of inspiration hit her. "I think he was worried that he was failing you, sir."

"He was," Hugo agreed shortly. He considered this answer for a moment. Fedotov had clearly hidden a great deal of things from him, and Hugo was regretting that the man was now dead. What else had he concealed?

"What progress did you make, Dr. Yordan?" He was trying to keep his voice harsh, which was not as easy as he had hoped with those pretty blue eyes staring at him. He looked down at the desk as she answered, trying to focus on her words.

"I had only recently arrived, sir. My research so far was simply to determine the nature of the problem."

Hugo noticed that she hesitated slightly before the last word. Interesting. "And what is the nature of the...*problem?*"

>>A Wechselbalg will observe different social mandates depending on their form.<< ADAM informed Jennifer. **>>Say it like that. Use academic language to throw him off.<<**

"A Wechselbalg will observe different social mandates depending on their form," Jennifer repeated.

Hugo only stared at her.

ADAM, come on, give me something else to work with.

>>In human form, a Wechselbalg is no more or less likely than any other human to resist torture techniques designed to ensure compliance. In wolf form, however, a Wechselbalg will instinctively act upon standing orders from the Alpha, so they will be unwilling to take orders from a third party. While there is a shared consciousness, and thus a shared emotional state between forms, a Wechselbalg will be less likely to be obedient to someone who is not their Alpha while they are in wolf form.<<

Jennifer repeated the words as quickly as she could while the language implant translated them to Spanish. After a few weeks spent trying to get herself to pronounce Bulgarian and Russian, she kept stumbling over the Spanish. She hoped that made things more believable, not less. Still, it was a disorienting act to play, and she was beginning to wonder how long she would be able to keep her cover.

Hugo, however, seemed interested. "I see." He settled back in his chair with a frown. "Were there any techniques that seemed to be especially useful?"

"I was still looking through the data on that, sir. There's limited evidence that it's simply a matter of time. Resistance will continue in wolf form after it has been exhausted in human form, but obedience will eventually be achieved. However, with so many individual cases and such a high failure rate—"

Hugo slammed his hand down on the desk. "What?"

"Which part, sir?" Jennifer let her voice quaver.

"A high failure rate?"

>>**Blame the administrator.**<< ADAM advised.

>>Hugo already hates him and he's dead anyway. He can't contradict you. Say you thought Hugo knew that the failure rate was that high.<<

ADAM, remind me never to get on your bad side.

"I thought you knew, sir." Jennifer swallowed, as if Hugo's anger worried her. Compared to literally anyone on Bethany Anne's team this guy was merely a little bitch, but he had to think he was terrifying. He had to believe in his own power for now, because that blinded him.

"Less than one in four Wechselbalg were successfully broken. One in four would die from their...injuries." She tried not to let her stomach heave as she repeated ADAM's words. "One half would rebel, and it was found that after they had attacked a scientist once, they would not stop doing so. They had to be eliminated."

She was going to be sick. She had seen so many battles at this point she thought death no longer troubled her, but it was one thing to die in battle. It was very different to be tortured and killed for trying to escape. To her relief, Hugo seemed not to want to discuss the matter further.

He leaned over the desk, black eyes boring into hers.

"Find the solution," he told her shortly. "One in four is not an acceptable success rate, and we do not have years to spend on every test subject. Find the way to make me their Alpha, and do it *quickly*. Those who fail me die. I did not make an exception for Fedotov, and I will not make one for you." He flicked his hand to dismiss her. "A car is waiting to take you to the facility. I will be waiting for your updates, Dr. Yordan."

Outside the room, Jennifer sagged against the wall and pressed a hand over her stomach.

"I hate this." Her murmur was so quiet that no one could have heard it except ADAM.

>>Would you like me to find you an escape route?<<

"No." Jennifer slowly pulled herself up, looking both ways down the hall before heading to her left. "No. I'm not going to run away." She told him, her mouth set in a firm line, "I'm going to destroy this."

2

Catalonia, Spain

"Thank you for coming." Hugo smiled across the table.

"Of course."

The woman smiling back at him was almost his exact opposite in terms of looks. Her white-blonde hair and pink lips were a testament to her Nordic heritage, and her skin was so pale that Hugo could see blue veins.

She wouldn't last very long in the Spanish sun.

Then again, she would not need to. Hugo would need deputies to rule over the pieces of Earth that were beyond his direct control. And he was beginning to recruit them—the last heirs of noble houses. Many simply laughed at him and told him that the age of kings and nobles had passed. Others, however, remembered the days when loyalty and family honor were the highest virtues. A time when they were not constrained by petty notions about peasants having rights. Where rulers were allowed to do whatever was necessary to bring order to the world.

This woman was one of them—Ranja Hallson, heir to a

family long thought extinct and relegated to the history books. The Danish nobility was only half-civilized at best in Hugo's opinion, having drunk honey spirits and worn fur pelts in smoky halls. But there was no denying their fighting prowess, and it was best to choose deputies that understood the lands they would rule.

The world was about to learn that the natural order could not be easily abolished.

"Tell me of your plan." Ranja took a sip of her wine and met Hugo's eyes. She saw his surprise at her direct words and did not bother to hide her satisfied smile. He had expected her to let him lead the conversation and not speak directly of the offer he had made—but she was direct by nature.

Not only that, she had seen the flicker of contempt in his eyes. He was about to learn that he would need a good plan and a good offer—a better one than he expected—to win her loyalty. Even then, when she had pledged fealty, he would learn that loyalty could not be bought so easily.

She saw no problem with accepting his gifts and his money and then turning her back if he began to give the wrong sorts of orders. He didn't know it, but his contempt was driving her price up. He thought his country was better simply because they had made stone castles instead of longhouses, because their food was different, and their winters were not so harsh. It was a ridiculous notion, and she would make him pay for it with good money—as well as access to the technology he supposedly had. He was, however, hesitating over revealing his plan. It was a bad sign in a potential ally.

Finally, he spoke.

"You have heard legends of shapeshifters, yes?"

Ranja frowned. "Fairy stories, yes. Witch's curses, usually—most of them feature bears." She saw the sudden flare of interest in Hugo's eyes and her frown deepened. "Why does it matter? Surely any country has stories like that about whatever animals live there."

"Perhaps," Hugo murmured. "And you have no stories of such animals moving in packs, their power transferred from generation to generation?"

Ranja kept her answer short. "No."

"Hmmm." Hugo considered, taking a bite of meat. It seemed that the curse of the Wechselbalg had spread across the globe, reaching far-flung corners, but what if accident or illness had wiped out some of the packs that *should* exist? He had hoped to use the native shapeshifters of each country for his plan, instead of being forced to use the limited resources of central and eastern Europe to control everything.

There were likely to be a number of uprisings at the start of his reign, and he had too few troops to put down all of them. But another possibility existed. Shapeshifters of the Nordic lands might have simply managed to conceal themselves better than those in the rest of Europe.

Who in their right mind, after all, would hunt down a bear the way one hunted down wolves that preyed on the livestock? It was a different order of magnitude. There was still hope.

"What if I were to tell you that such myths were not uncommon across Europe and Asia?" Hugo raised an eyebrow and took another sip of his wine.

"You mean werewolves?" Ranja gave him a patronizing smile. "I hardly think—"

Hugo pressed a button, and a curtain slid open along one wall. The moving curtain did not reveal a window to that outside, as Ranja had assumed, but a reinforced glass window showing an examination room. A man was chained in the center, clothed in loose black pants and a shirt.

Hugo pressed another button, and the man began to writhe as if in pain.

Ranja recoiled. This man thought the longhouses and furs of the Danes were uncivilized, and he was showing her torture with her dinner? But as she readied herself to spit curses at him and leave, movement caught the corner of her eye. Her mouth dropped open. A wolf stood where a man had moments before, and it lowered its head and snarled at her through the glass. She walked around the table to lay her hand on the window and smiled when it snapped at her.

Her people had been warriors once, and she knew another warrior when she saw one.

"As you can see," Hugo continued softly, "these are more than just rumors. The myths are *true*. If you find such shapeshifters in your own lands, I will teach you to turn them into an army—and give you all of Denmark to rule."

QBS *ArchAngel*

"Ranja Hallson," Lance Reynolds began as they walked. He held out a tablet displaying a picture. "Danish royalty of a sort, from way back."

"Huh." Bethany Anne adjusted the hem of her jacket and raised an eyebrow. "What do we know about this woman? I don't remember hearing her name before."

"You wouldn't have. She hasn't been on our radar—or anyone else's. I had ADAM run a search on her, and she's not flagged by the Danish government, the US, the UK, or INTERPOL." Lance flipped through the pages of blank searches on his screen. "You name it; they don't give a damn about her."

"So why does Hugo Marcari?" Bethany Anne's confusion was evident.

"Because he's an ideologue." Lance sighed and rubbed his forehead. When he left the Army, he'd thought he was done with fighting religious zealots hell-bent on binding the entire world to their vision.

Apparently, he'd been wrong.

Shouts reached their ears, echoing down the hallway from the area right outside the landing bay. Both of them looked up with a frown.

"What's that?" Bethany Anne asked.

"I'm not sure."

"It sounds like Peter." Bethany Anne quickened her pace. "Back to Hugo for a moment. How did ADAM know about the meeting?"

"Oh." Lance's face broke into a broad smile. "ADAM has managed to work his way into almost all of Hugo's systems. Each research facility maintains an independent server for their work, and so does his headquarters. Stephen doesn't want to hear it, but it's only because Jennifer was there that we know where it is. Apparently, ADAM is helping her get bugs into the headquarters system to locate all the other facilities and take down their security systems. Hugo seems to hold all his meetings in rooms without security cameras, but we have access to most of his communications. After the meeting with Ranja he sent her a very simple message, stating only that he looked forward to doing business if she could find the appropriate resources."

"What do you suppose *that* refers to?" Bethany Anne's eyes narrowed in speculation. "Have ADAM look over their shipping manifests. I want to know if he's buying a lot of anything in particular and its purpose. The research, maybe?"

"Possibly," Lance agreed. "He's compiling a report on the methodology used, but he's been reticent. It seems that his analysis distressed Jennifer."

"He's been in contact with her?" Bethany Anne felt a wave of relief. She'd known that contact with ADAM was the plan, but it was good to hear that the plan was working.

"Fairly constant contact. I guess Hugo was smart enough to question her when she arrived, and ADAM provided a cover story." Lance chuckled. "In addition to helping her pretend she speaks Spanish."

"So Stephen should be feeling better, yes?" Bethany Anne asked with an eyebrow raised.

"Not at all. I'm not sure ADAM's told him about this conversation, in fact. When Stephen found out Jennifer had gone on Hugo's helicopter because ADAM said he could help her pretend to be a scientist, Stephen was *not* happy."

"Well, I'll explain to ADAM that when one of my team asks a question, it's usually because they have an incredibly stupid idea they want to pursue." Bethany Anne chewed her lip. "I'll talk to Stephen about it, but I don't think he's really angry at ADAM."

"No," Lance agreed quietly. "If I know Stephen I wouldn't think he's even angry, not really."

The two of them came around the corner and stopped abruptly.

"Because he should have known something like this would happen!" Peter's roar traveled down the corridor. "He should have planned for it! He shouldn't have let her get on that *Gott Verdammt* helicopter alone!"

Stephen stood with his arms crossed, leaning against a wall. Nathan stood between him and Peter.

"She's part of our team," Nathan told Peter. His voice was even, but there was a warning there. "You would have done the same thing."

"She's a warrior," Stephen interjected quietly. "She is every bit as capable as you or Nathan of being on Bethany Anne's team. She wouldn't be here if she wasn't."

"Here on Bethany Anne's team, or here on the ship?" Peter shot back. "You know the answer. She would be *here* with us instead of leaving the fight to get on that asslicking psychopath's helicopter to who knows where!"

"That was not weakness as a fighter. It was a tactical choice." Stephen was clearly struggling to keep his voice level.

"She should never have been there in the first place," Peter interrupted. "You should have called in the Bitches instead."

"Peter," Nathan snarled, "shut up before I shut you up."

"No! No Wechselbalg should have had to go in there. But no, *he* wanted to bring his girlfriend—"

"I didn't want her there either!" Stephen yelled back. "You think I wanted her to see that? I kept her out of the facility at Sofia, and I tried to keep her from going to Velingrad!"

"Well, that clearly worked fantastically," Peter snapped, not noticing Bethany Anne gliding up to them.

"Everybody just *SHUT THE FUCK UP!*" she yelled.

All three men fell silent and Lance raised his eyebrows and crossed his arms over his chest, then took two steps so he could lean against the wall.

This was about to get interesting.

"All three of you," Bethany Anne continued carefully, anger simmering in her voice, "care for Jennifer. And while all three of you want to keep her from danger as friends, Stephen and Nathan seem to have realized that this isn't what's expected of my team. Do I need to refresh your memory, Peter? That people on *my* team fight, they don't hang back and let someone else do the dirty work. They know they're in it together. The people on *my* team know that they will go into danger for a higher purpose. Has it occurred to you that Jennifer knew we would make use of the information she was providing, not only to take down our enemy but also get her out?"

All three men stared at her silently. Peter looked away first.

"Jennifer," Bethany Anne continued, her voice still deathly soft, "made a choice to infiltrate Hugo's operation. It was a high-stakes choice. It was a dangerous choice. But it was not necessarily a bad choice—and it was *her* choice to make. I might have done the same, given her capabilities and the opportunity. I appreciate the fact that we now have the location of two of Hugo's facilities, including his headquarters. Jennifer gave us an opportunity we would not have otherwise had, and for that I am grateful.

"Meanwhile, the three of you need to accept that she's in danger and will be in danger again after we leave Earth. *All of us will*. Every one of you has faced death in my service." Her nod included John. "We'll get her back, and we will make Hugo pay. Jennifer's work will help us make that happen. In the meantime, I will not accept fighting on my team." She took a moment to eye each man, "Are we clear?"

The three men nodded.

"All of you go decompress, and try to keep the blood off the carpets," Bethany Anne went to the door, then shot them a look over her shoulder. "We need to put together a strategy and get you back to Earth. We have an opportunity to hit Hugo where it hurts, and we can't waste it."

Catalonia, Spain

Gerard ducked under his opponent's swing and the blow glanced off his shoulder. He grunted as he drove his fist into the man's solar plexus, and when his opponent stumbled and fell to his knees Gerard seized his opportunity. Most people would have stopped, but Gerard was not "most people."

A flurry of punches caught his opponent around the head and neck and he was prone on the floor a moment later.

Gerard stepped back as servants hurried forward to lift the man's unconscious body out of the ring. It had been a good round. He always fought best when he was thinking, and he always thought best when he was training.

It was a different pleasure than his work punishing those who failed Hugo, and far more visceral. It was one of the only places in his life that he allowed pain to be his teacher rather than his tool. He also thought privately that it made him a better adviser to Hugo.

His employer had grown up with private tutors who had taught the classic texts on philosophy and strategy. He had learned the nuances of chess, and his tutors had helped him dissect the major battles of world history. But no one had ever dared to strike Hugo Marcari, so no one had taught him to use his fists. Gerard had nothing but respect for Hugo's expertise in certain areas, but someone who had never been in a fight couldn't really understand tactics and strategy.

Gerard never stressed this advantage. He had become very good at suggesting contradictory courses of action without Hugo even noticing. Hugo liked to believe the ideas he executed were his and his alone, and Gerard was content enough in Hugo's service to let the man believe that.

But right now, he was convinced Hugo was making a mistake.

The attack on TQB's offices in Spain had been too rash and too early. Hugo still believed that as soon as he showed his strength the common people of the world would flock behind him. Gerard did not believe that—and he worried that the attack had tipped their hand.

What if TQB learned of Hugo's plan before he had enough allies to take them on? Gerard had even floated the idea of letting TQB leave Earth forever—as it was rumored they would—and simply take over after they were gone. Hugo had rejected the idea out of hand.

For him to win, he reasoned, someone *else* must lose.

Gerard grimaced and settled into his fighting stance as another opponent came into the ring—Marcelo, the guard captain of Hugo's main estate. The two men crouched and began to circle.

Hugo's approach was flawed, Gerard thought. These blind spots were a problem for him, and thus a problem for Gerard.

His thoughts faltered as a lunge from Marcelo narrowly missed. He always underestimated this man's speed. Gerard shifted away, staying light on his feet, his eyes fixed on the other man's sternum. For a boxer, every motion began there.

Of course, while he had started with boxing, he had long since outgrown the strict rules of that fighting form. In fighting, Gerard believed there *were* no rules.

He deflected another attack with a knee to Marcelo's thigh and the two men broke apart to circle again.

His mind was racing. He was convinced that at least one of the women they had brought with them was not who she seemed to be.

He had studied everything he could on Hsu, but there were no records at all of Irina Yordan. The only references he could find online showed a woman who was not the same at all. There had been a prisoner named Irina, but this was clearly not the same person.

What was the key? How could he find out? Gerard absorbed a hit from Marcelo and hissed in pain, lashing out with his elbow reflexively.

With no solution in sight, his fighting skills were suffering. And then it came to him, and without a conscious thought his fist lashed out to catch Marcelo on the cheek. His foot followed with a kick to drive the man back.

If either Hsu or Irina was the double agent, they would be weak.

Gerard had learned that only the strongest could do what it took to serve Hugo. That was why Gerard remained one of the man's few confidants. He advanced on Marcelo, unmercifully raining blows on the man's back as the guard captain raised his hands feebly to protect his head. Only when the man was out cold did Gerard stop.

He was breathing heavily, but he was smiling.

He would play the two women off one another. One of them was sure to break, and then he would know who was trying to infiltrate Hugo's operation.

3

QBS ArchAngel

"You may begin speaking," a calm voice told Irina in Bulgarian.

"Where should I look?" She craned her neck to glance around the room. Nothing in this conference room looked like speakers, and she was nervous about speaking to ADAM. She had been introduced, of course—if one could call it that when there was no one to see or shake hands with—but something about the lack of inflection made her nervous. It was a computer.

Was it really alive?

"It doesn't matter where you look. I have no location," ADAM informed her.

"Great," Irina muttered. "That makes me feel better."

"If you would like to speak to someone else, you are welcome to do so." The words would have been sarcastic in a human, but she sensed that the AI meant them literally. "I offered to speak with you because it might be easier for you to tell your story without observing a listener's reactions."

It would make her look like a crazy person to speak to no one, but Irina supposed the AI wouldn't care. "Thank you, ADAM."

The AI admitted, "It was not my idea. I was surprised to learn that this would be a consideration."

Were all AIs so scrupulously honest? Irina found herself smiling, against all odds. ADAM was beginning to grow on her. "Well, then, thank you for taking the advice. Um, where do you want me to start? I just want to get this over with."

She didn't want to do it at all, really, but she knew she must. Her information might help them figure out what Hugo was trying to do, and reverse it. No one ever said that. In fact, they had gone out of their way to *avoid* saying it. She knew they were trying to keep from giving her false hope.

But Irina hadn't been able to stop thinking about the mind-controlled Wechselbalg in the Velingrad facility. She wasn't sure she could bear to fight any more of them. If they *could* undo what had been done...

"Tell us what you can remember about how you were captured," ADAM suggested, breaking her reverie. "And go from there."

"Okay." She cleared her throat nervously. "I had gone to Sofia to track down a family member from our pack who went missing while on vacation. I told my pack leader I was going and he..." Her throat closed. "He threw me out of the pack. I knew he was going to do that, though. Out of respect for pack rules, when I found a lead on the family, I didn't contact anyone. I had met a man who said he might know where they had gone. He wanted to meet me somewhere public, so I didn't think I would be in danger. But after he told me about the facility in the mountains, he had me followed and they captured me in the forest. They shot me with a poisoned silver-tipped arrow."

She shuddered at the memory. She had been writhing on the ground, the pain consuming her...and then the poison had begun to work. Her eyes dropped. She had barely seen the figures who came to carry her away, and though she managed to get a good hit in, she was no match for them in her poisoned condition.

When she woke, she was in a cage.

"When they brought you to the facility, what was the first thing they did?" ADAM's voice was impersonal. That actually helped, Irina decided. She couldn't imagine telling Stoyan this. It would cause him pain, and she wouldn't know what to say to comfort him.

"They put a tracking chip in me; in my upper arm." Irina pointed to the place. She healed well enough that there was no scar where Hsu had cut it out of her, but she still remembered.

"They did not put in any other chips?"

"No. Why?"

There was a pause.

"ADAM?"

"I am not certain if I am supposed to share this with you. If you become distressed, you may not remember things as clearly."

"Yes, but now I know you're hiding something."

"Humans are impossible," ADAM muttered.

Irina managed a smile. "Please tell me why you asked."

"The wolves we brought back from Velingrad had chips implanted at the base of the skull. I can see that you do not have such a chip now, but I was not sure if you had removed it yourself."

"No." Irina shook her head in confusion. "I didn't...I didn't know."

"That was either a later stage of the experiment or something that was particular to the Velingrad facility," ADAM explained. "Please, go on."

Irina's body shook as she spoke. She told ADAM everything, pressing on when her voice broke and refused to respond when he questioned her well-being. She recounted every detail she could remember. She was now driven by one urge only: make sure that what had happened to her would never happen to anyone else. *Ever.*

Outside the room, Stoyan leaned his head against the wall.

"Stoyan?" Arisha wavered. She knew that in some ways it wasn't her place to take him away from here, but she could also see the issue more clearly than he could. "Irina is telling her story to ADAM because she doesn't want you to be hurt, knowing what happened to her."

"But it *did* happen!" Stoyan caught himself just before he slammed his fist into the wall. He hissed, "Hiding from it does nothing."

"And listening to the story doesn't change it," Arisha argued fiercely. "She's here. She's safe. You heard her say she knew what she was doing when she went to Sofia. Why do you need to hear this? Is it just to punish yourself for not being there? Because if so, you're not doing anybody any good."

Stoyan looked at her. He did not know what to say to this fierce diatribe. Part of him wanted to tell Arisha to leave him alone. He wanted to tell her she didn't understand what was going on or how this felt. But he also knew the truth; she was right.

All he was doing was punishing himself by listening to a story he could not change.

"What should I—" He broke off; he had to stop asking that question. He was not an Alpha yet—perhaps he never would be—but he knew that he might need to lead a group again, so he had to learn to make his own decisions. He tried to smile and gestured down the hall. "You're right. Let's walk. I am feeling a bit stir-crazy in here."

"But it's so big!" Arisha looked around herself with a laugh. "It's just like being in a building, isn't it?"

"A building with no windows," Stoyan grumbled. "No live air. No trees. When you're a Wechselbalg, you perceive the world through smell as well as with your eyes. This place smells unnatural to me. I can smell living things, but also much metal. It makes my nose itch."

Arisha laughed. "Well, maybe we'll go back to Earth soon. In fact, I was thinking I might go to Spain."

Stoyan looked at her sharply. "On your own?"

"Why not?" Her look challenged him.

"Oh, I don't know." He looked up at the ceiling in mock ignorance as they strolled. "I'm not sure I can think of any reasons, beyond, you know, the fact that our enemy is there. With all his bodyguards, and that bastard who likes to torture people."

"Gerard is why I'm going, actually." Arisha twisted her hands.

"You're kidding me."

"No, I'm serious. He's still the weak link. I'm not sure if he's more insane than Hugo, but he goes out more than Hugo does and it's easy to tempt him."

"And you think you can take this guy out on your own?"

"It's not like I'm going to challenge him to a duel."

"I wasn't worried about you two dueling, I was worried about him torturing you to death," Stoyan ground out. "Look, you're not my pack, I don't have any authority over you."

"I thought you weren't the Alpha." Arisha frowned.

"A pack doesn't run entirely on an Alpha's orders," Stoyan told her, amused. "There are certain rules of behavior. Basically, you don't put yourself in danger needlessly, because if you die the pack gets weaker."

She paused a moment. "Oh. I hadn't thought of that."

"Seriously, how do humans survive?" Stoyan shook his head. "It's a complete mystery to me."

"Yeah, yeah." Arisha paused. "Wait. You don't want me to put myself in danger because you think of me as part of your pack, kind of. Right?"

Stoyan looked away, rubbing the back of his neck. He was suddenly far too hot and far too aware of the woman looking at him. He was worried that he might be blushing. *Warriors*, he thought desperately, *did not blush*.

He was *definitely* blushing.

"I think of *you* as part of *my* pack," Arisha offered. Her voice sounded unusually high. "I mean, as much as I understand those things. I know that I don't really get it, but I still want to help."

"Stoyan, she continued. "I'm not thinking of going to Spain because I have a death wish, or I want to be brave. I'm going because I might be able to help us stop Hugo. I'm not a scientist, so I can't undo what his scientists did. I'm not a warrior, so I can't assault the bases like you can. But I'm really good at getting people to slip up and tell me things. I know pack members aren't supposed to endanger themselves needlessly, but aren't they supposed to be willing to accept danger in order to help each other?"

Stoyan looked at her and her expression warmed his chest. He'd never met a woman like this. "Yeah." He knew he was smiling—and he couldn't stop. "Yeah, that's right." He took a deep breath. He was more nervous than he could ever recall feeling. "Uh, Arisha…"

Her eyes were very wide. "Yes?"

"You're like no one I've ever met before. That is to say, uh…well… I'm really no good at this. What I *mean* is…"

A few hundred yards away, Lance's earpiece buzzed.

>>**Lance?**<<

"Yes?"

>>**They just kissed. I win the bet.**<<

"Goddammit." Lance let out a sigh. Was it just his imagination, or had ADAM figured out how to sound smug?

"What's your plan?" Peter dropped into a chair and looked at Nathan, who was bouncing his daughter in his arms.

Peter's rooms were very Spartan. He didn't own much beyond his military gear, and he liked it that way. He'd found a purpose in serving Bethany Anne that he'd never had before.

His old life—cluttered with possessions like expensive jackets and motorcycles—no longer appealed to him.

At present, however, the room had been entirely taken over by Christina Bethany Anne Lowell. Bethany Anne had brought not only Peter with her for this trip, but also Ecaterina and Christina. Even though she weighed mere pounds, and was just visiting, the diaper bag, blankets, and toys had somehow spread everywhere.

Nathan was walking up and down while bouncing her gently.

"I think I'm going to pay a visit to Bulgaria," Nathan told him. "I want…" He lost his train of thought and smiled down at the baby in his arms, then cooed at her when she started to fuss.

Peter waited patiently. He'd seen a few new parents over the years, so he knew it was useless to try to get their attention back at this stage of the game. Infants had a primal hold on their parents. It was one of the few things that matched pack loyalty in terms of instinct and strength.

"Ah." Nathan remembered himself and cleared his throat hastily. "Sorry. Right. I want to pay a visit to Stoyan and Irina's Alpha. Well, former Alpha. I want to try to make him understand."

Peter frowned in confusion. "Understand what?"

"Times are changing." Nathan sat carefully, his

daughter now fast asleep with her head on his shoulder. "The things that used to keep us safe and the ways we used to escape notice—well, they don't work anymore. The world is more interconnected, too. All these people are coming to join Bethany Anne because they understand that the old petty infighting isn't helping us. The leaders don't see it, though, and unfortunately that goes for Wechselbalg too. Stoyan's Alpha is thinking of the short-term; of keeping his pack members out of Hugo's research facilities. He isn't thinking of the long-term. He doesn't get that Hugo's just the first person to try to do this."

Peter nodded, sinking his chin into one hand as he thought. One of the things that made Nathan a great adviser, Second to his Alpha back on Earth and now to Bethany Anne, was his ability to see past the issue at hand to the heart of the matter—the issues that rippled out to the wider world.

He saw no benefit in isolation.

"I feel bad for him," Nathan admitted.

"The Alpha?"

Nathan nodded. "Yes, in a way. He made a foolish choice because he didn't go looking for allies. He knew they couldn't assault the facility on their own and win, so he forbade his pack from having anything to do with it. It was a bad decision. He should have known they wouldn't just accept it when it meant that their family and friends were going to be left behind. But I understand what it is to realize the world has changed and not know how to deal with that." Nathan shook his head slightly. His eyes were unfocused as he rested a hand lovingly on his daughter's back. "He needs to understand we can't keep doing things the old way. It won't work."

"And you think you can convince him of that?" Peter wasn't so sure it could be done. He'd seen a lot of Wechselbalg turn up their noses at that kind of thinking.

"Worked for you, didn't it?" Nathan flashed him a grin.

"Now, that's not entirely accurate," Peter pointed out. "I was also a whiny bastard. Everyone knew it, even me."

Nathan choked on a laugh, trying to stay silent so as not to wake his daughter.

Peter continued, "I'm just saying, it's going to be harder to convince an Alpha who has successfully—I know, not really successfully, but just go with it—led his pack for years than it was to convince a whiny little bitch that he needed to man up."

"I know." Nathan sobered a little. He was rocking back and forth as his daughter stirred, trying to get her back to sleep. "But I have to try. You know that's how Bethany Anne does things. People have to be given a chance to do the right thing."

"If we try to give every individual a chance, we're going to talk ourselves hoarse," Peter replied. "And besides, we don't have the time."

"Okay, true. If he won't listen that's on him, but I want to give him a chance." Nathan shook his head. "I hate the idea that we're leaving Wechselbalg behind on this world. What happens when we're not here anymore to break into facilities and free the experiments? They have to start thinking differently or everyone we leave behind is going to suffer."

>>Lance, there's a news report you should see.<<

"What is it? Show me." Lance looked at the video ADAM displayed on the wall and frowned at the images. As far as he could tell, there wasn't much to see. A few police chiefs across Europe had been killed, mostly in Eastern bloc countries. He imagined that sort of thing wasn't all that uncommon.

"What am I looking at, ADAM?"

>>All six of these men were killed in the same way within hours of one another, and all of them are in towns that have rented land or a derelict factory for scientific research.<<

Lance gave a low whistle. "Well, I'll be. Do we know anything more?"

>>It's not clear right now who did it. Perhaps we should send someone to ask around. It's possible that the police chiefs were trafficking Wechselbalg and the local packs had them assassinated, or that they were thinking of enforcing some laws and Hugo had them assassinated. Either way, it may provide us with the rest of the locations where Hugo has facilities.<<

"No luck on finding that out through the computer systems?"

>>Not yet.<<

"If we just cut the head off the snake..." Lance mused.

>>If I understand your analogy correctly, you mean to eliminate Hugo as a first step, yes?<<

"Yes."

>>I am not certain that this tactic would be effective

in our present situation. Hugo's facilities operate with a high degree of autonomy. The chances are too high either that their research would continue or that they would kill the experiments and flee.<<

"This is a mess." Lance rubbed his forehead. "Nathan is going back to Bulgaria to speak to Stoyan's pack and I think we should have him look into this. I'm going to go talk to Bethany Anne. The media doesn't love us right now, but what if we could get them evidence of what Hugo is doing?"

>>I do not have much personal experience with humans compared to many here, but I think that may backfire.<<

"Yeah, I should probably stop expecting people to be reasonable, shouldn't I?" Lance put on his jacket and left the room. "Guess this means we just have to do this the old-fashioned way."

I'm not sure I follow, TOM interjected.

"Get to the root of the problem and kill it—thoroughly. Hugo, his headquarters, and every one of those facilities." Lance whistled cheerily. "I tell ya, TOM, this guy really has it coming."

Bethany Anne stood alone on the observation deck of the ship, looking down at the curve of the Earth below. It glowed, beautiful and untroubled from this distance.

She wished she had faith in that illusion.

May I ask what you're thinking about? TOM queried.

She rubbed her forehead. *Why?*

Because every time I think I understand humans in the context of Kurtherians, you surprise me.

Bethany Anne smiled. *Now, TOM, don't tell me anything is beyond your comprehension. I may start to doubt you.*

Humans are frequently illogical.

Yes, Mr. Spock, I know. She let out a breath as she stared at the planet.

I do not understand why you are not getting involved personally. Do you not feel capable of resolving this quickly?

I could, easily. I want to. She clenched her hands and tried to relax. *But this is Stephen's operation. It's his problem to fix, and this team needs to run the operation on their own.*

Your vocal patterns suggest that you're not sure about this course of action.

Every day you get a little more like ADAM, Bethany Anne muttered.

His way of looking at the world has a certain elegance.

Uh-huh. Look, TOM. I'm human. Earth will always be home, in a way. Bethany Anne admitted. *And it pisses me off to watch people screwing with it. I hate that people like Hugo seem to just get away with whatever they want, and when I try to help people everyone falls all over each other to stop me.* She shook her head. *I said I was going to leave Earth alone for a while, and I meant it. It's just hard not to intervene when they're doing things like this.*

So why don't you intervene?

Because I have faith in my team. I have faith that they can shut this down quickly and effectively, and that's not blind faith. I've seen them in action. I was impressed by how they took down Velingrad. Meanwhile, if I don't prepare for what's through that Gate, there might not be a world for them to mess up anymore. Bethany Anne straightened up and nodded decisively. *So back to work, TOM. We have a lot to do.* She strode across the room, footsteps echoing in the silence. *TOM?*

Bobcat, Marcus, and William are requesting transportation from the *Meredith Reynolds*.

Why?

They say they want to be on Earth for the extraction of your shoes.

On the ArchAngel?

On Earth.

That's odd. What could they be planning?

I'm not certain, although from what I've heard William would like to visit Belgium and Bobcat has been researching Spanish hops.

Bethany Anne snorted. *I should have known it would be about beer. I'll go get them. They can do whatever they want as long as they don't foul up Stephen's mission—or forget my shoes.*

She shook her head fondly, straightened her cuffs, and vanished into the Etheric.

4

Sofia, Bulgaria

"Ow! Fuck." Tabitha skidded across the cement floor covered with glass shards and broken equipment, rolled, and stood up with a frown. "That fucking *hurt*."

Ryu dropped onto the floor in an elegant crouch. "Maybe you should work on your landings?"

"Maybe *you* should…" Tabitha thought for a moment, annoyed. "I don't know. I don't have any follow up to that." Tabitha jabbed a finger at Hirotoshi as he joined Ryu. "And don't *you* start, either."

"Of course not." Hirotoshi swept an elegant bow. "Lead on, Kemosabe."

Tabitha muttered, "That is exactly the sort of thing I was talking about." She climbed over the piles of rubble, adjusting her black jacket and gloves as she went. All black, comfortable as all get out, and easy to fight in—this outfit was her dream—not to mention her ass looked great in it. She tossed a look over her shoulder at it and grinned. "*Damn*, I look good."

"Where is the server room?" Ryu asked.

"Do you mind? I'm having a moment, here." Tabitha complained and tapped her wrist.

"Stephen? Do you know where the server room is?"

"Southeast corner of the castle." Stephen's voice was abrupt. "Bottom floor."

Tabitha had been warned by Barnabas that Stephen was out of sorts due to Jennifer taking a solo mission. She rolled her eyes. He needed to man up, in her opinion. Jennifer was going to be fine. If she got caught at the facility where she was pretending to be a scientist, she could just fight her way out.

Tabitha was even a little bit jealous. When she imagined Jennifer filling out a lab coat, spitting out equations and scientific phrases while the rest of the scientists just stared at her, it was all Tabitha could do not to laugh.

She took two steps to the edge of the pile of rubble and jumped. "Here we gooooo!" There was a noise below. "Fuck, *ow!*"

Ryu muttered, "I told her, right?" He scouted the distance to the ground and followed her down.

He turned to look as Hirotoshi followed him. "Seriously, *you* heard me, right?"

"Normally, I would say the problem would fix itself." Hirotoshi looked on as Tabitha scowled at a swiftly-healing laceration on her arm. "But in this case, I think we should accept it as a consistent state of affairs."

"I *heard* that." Tabitha glared at them. "Come on. This place sucks."

"We want to hit both sets of servers," Stephen reminded

her. *The ones that sent information to Hugo's headquarters and the ones that were not connected.*

"Yeah, I remember." Tabitha rolled her eyes as she trotted along the hallway. "What happened to this place, anyway?"

"They bombed it."

"No shit?"

"Yes. I was here at the time."

"Good job not getting blown up." Men, in Tabitha's opinion, seemed to need praise. Accordingly, she made an effort to dole it out.

"Thank you," Stephen replied drily. "I wasn't sure the mission was a success until just now."

"I was trying to be nice." Tabitha heaved a fallen door out of the way and stepped back as a pile of rubble fell. She clambered over it and her eyes picked up a staircase leading down into the dark. "Am I heading in the right direction?"

"Yes."

"You know, I don't know what you're so upset about," she told him as she stepped over more crap that was in her way.

"Here it comes," Hirotoshi whispered to Ryu as they followed Tabitha down the stairs.

"I am not talking about this with you," Stephen told her simply.

"It's not like you wouldn't have done the same thing if you had thought of it," Tabitha pressed. "I mean, she probably had a better chance of pulling it off because of the tits and all—"

"I said, I am not discussing this with you."

"But if you'd had the foresight to get into that helicopter and con them, you totally would have. And she would have been totally cool with it." There was deafening silence from the other end of the line. "Hello?"

Ryu and Hirotoshi shifted uncomfortably and winced when Tabitha punched a metal door leading to the lowest basement level. When it still didn't move, she wrenched it off its hinges and dropped it, then smacked the alarm pad which was beginning to flash red.

"Hate those things. It's the one time I regret the aural implants." She went down the stairs. "I know you're still there, Stephen. Ah ha! Server room."

"I am still here, yes."

"Aren't you going to say anything?"

"There is nothing to say. You are not as familiar with me as you might think, and—"

"I knew it." Tabitha threw a glance over her shoulder at the two guys and began to plug in uplink drives. "I touched a nerve."

"I would not have just run off without—"

"*Definitely* touched a nerve."

Since Stephen couldn't see them, Hirotoshi and Ryu nodded.

QBS ArchAngel

"What are you picking up?" Marcus looked over William's shoulder at the laptop screen.

"Hey!" William jerked the laptop away. "Competitive classified information. Don't you look at my hop mix." William had spent the past two weeks coming up with it, and the best part was an ingredient he could get only in Catalonia—where they would be landing shortly to get the shoes.

He planned to sneak off to buy it, and he didn't want either of his brothers from other mothers profiting from his research.

Marcus tried again. "Oh, come on, you can show me."

"Stop trying to look or I'll pour salt in your beer!" William growled.

"Gentlemen." Lance looked at them. "We have more important matters to attend to."

"You're the one who proposed the competition," William pointed out.

"Indeed. Having read the incident reports from various countries, I am also fairly familiar with my daughter's temper. I would not fail to get her those shoes. That is presently your first priority."

"Right." Marcus pulled out his laptop. "So, France, huh?"

"They are in an unsecured depot in the mountains." Lance gave them a look. "You'd better come up with a good way to find, mute, or otherwise deal with any tracking devices that may have been put in there in the meantime. And God help us all if they've gotten moldy or something."

All of the men shuddered.

"And anyway," Bobcat reminded the other two. "You don't really need to worry about this competition, because neither of you will ever out-brew me."

"I wouldn't be so sure about that." Lance raised his eyebrows. "Think about your competition. Think about *Barnabas* being part of your competition."

"Are you trying to scare me?" Bobcat asked.

"No, not at all." Lance smiled. "I'm trying to make sure you all bring your A game so I have a lot of good beer to drink."

Catalonia, Spain

Jacobo Dominguez came into the break room to find someone hastily hiding olives, bread, and a bottle of wine under a table.

"Oh, it's you." Telmo pulled the bottle back out and held it out to him. "I thought it was that sonofabitch."

The other men groaned in commiseration.

Since Hugo had returned that afternoon Gerard had been inspecting everything. He'd been heard arguing with the guard captain about patrol routes and the responses to break-ins at the facility and headquarters. The answer that there hadn't ever been any had been insufficient; the guard captain was now walking with a limp.

Everyone tried not to notice that.

It wasn't just the patrol routes, either. Gerard seemed, suddenly, to know things he shouldn't have any way of knowing—secret affairs, who went into the town to get drunk, and who talked shit about Hugo. A few of the guard were simply gone now, and the rest knew they should keep quiet—but it was hard not to hate that guy.

"Did you hear the newest thing?" Telmo gave Jacobo a meaningful look.

"No. Do I want to?" He took a sip of the wine and passed it back. "This is shit. You couldn't get something good to make it worth our while?"

"You buy next time, then." Telmo was unrepentant. "He warned us off that new scientist."

Jacobo didn't need to ask who he meant. Word had spread like wildfire about the scientist Hugo had brought back with him—Irina, someone had said. She filled out a lab coat like nothing else, and Telmo liked to say there was something dangerous about her. Telmo was strange like that, but even Jacobo had to admit that there was more to her than just the toned body. It was something about the way she watched a room, paused before she spoke, and tried not to mingle with the other scientists.

Hugo had apparently questioned her, himself, or so the story went. Jacobo thought that maybe he'd tried to talk the woman out of staying. After all, the research here was...unpleasant. Maybe he'd offered her a place up at headquarters, instead. But whatever he'd said, Gerard hung around her all of the time. He asked about her. He wanted to know where she went and who she worked with—as if the lab logs wouldn't show him. Jacobo supposed that this was the next logical step.

He suggested, "Maybe he wants her for himself."

There was a round of knowing looks that suggested they'd discussed this already and come to the same conclusion.

"Yeah." Telmo leaned forward. "Told us, not a single word to her or we'd be thrown out of here with no pension and he'd make sure we never worked again."

Jacobo whistled. "Well, it's not worth my job to get shot down, eh, guys?"

There was a burst of laughter and a few men clapped him on the back.

Outside the door, Gerard shook his head in disappointment. The failures at Sofia and Velingrad had shown him that conventional methods were not working to keep the staff focused and productive. He'd spent the past weeks searching through personal details of each staff member here, trying to find and root out any signs of the trouble that had led to catastrophe at those facilities. He wished Hugo hadn't cleared that woman. He turned and made his way down the hallway, then out into the blazing afternoon sun. It would be a long climb to the castle, but he wanted to be alone. He didn't trust himself around anyone else right now, even a driver.

His hands clenched. Hugo kept messing up, and it always fell to Gerard to pick up the pieces. The new scientist was trouble, why couldn't he see it? Her work could hardly be useful enough to risk another facility. Let the men think that he wanted her all to himself. He didn't care, just as long as they stayed away from her and out of whatever trouble she was spinning.

Lonely men—and all of the guards here were lonely— could be talked into anything. Like letting someone into a facility. Like looking away while someone stole all their data. Like letting the experiments out.

She needed to go. And since Hugo clearly wasn't going to help, Gerard would need to make his own plan.

"ADAM, do you want to tell me what the hell I'm staring at?" Jennifer frowned down at the document in front of her. It might as well be written in gibberish, for all the sense it made to her, and Dr. Molinero would be back all too soon to ask about her progress. He'd handed her the stack of papers almost the moment she walked in the door and told her he wanted her opinion within the hour.

She was tired, she was jet-lagged, and she wanted a damned bath.

>>I can never be entirely certain with humans, but I believe his request was not entirely genuine<<

"What do you mean?" Jennifer felt a prickle on the back of her neck.

>>Given what you stated to Hugo as your area of expertise, you would likely not be familiar with immunology<<

"He's just seeing if I'll admit that I don't know what he's talking about?"

>>Yes. I believe the other scientists are unhappy with the fact that Hugo has given you such a prominent role, when you're a newcomer<<

"Well, they can just get over it," Jennifer snapped. She lowered her voice to subvocalization again. "I'm not trying to put anyone out of a job."

>>In all fairness, you are.<<

"Oh. Yeah. Oops. But I'm not trying to, you know...take anyone's spot."

>>Somehow, I don't think that will be a comfort to them<< ADAM pointed out.

"And you know how they could avoid that problem? Not doing experiments on Wechselbalg." Despite the fact that she wasn't sure if the *ArchAngel* was currently overhead, she shot a triumphant glance skywards. "Boom. Logic."

Footsteps sounded in the hallway outside, however, and she swore under her breath.

"What do I do about this? ADAM, help!"

>>**Just tell him it's not your area of expertise, and he should know that**<<

"Hmm." Jennifer looked down at the papers, and then a slow smile spread across her face. "*Or*...we could mess with him."

>>**How do you mean**<<

"You understand this, right?"

>>**Yes, I researched it extensively when he brought you the papers**<<

"Then let's pretend I *do* know what I'm talking about. Please, tell me there are errors on here."

>>**Numerous errors**<< ADAM assured her.

"Good. I'm going to point them out."

>>**I don't understand what we're doing.**<<

"Think of it like a pack," Jennifer advised. "He tried to assert dominance over me. The correct answer to that isn't to just ignore that attempt. It's to assert dominance over *him*. Get it?"

>>**No, but I'll take your word for it. Can I talk to TOM about this?**<<

"Sure, whatever." The doorknob turned. "Get ready." Jennifer directed a brilliant smile in the direction of Dr. Molinero. "Hello again, Doctor."

"Hello." The man had a predatory smile on his face. Tall and thin, with what seemed like unnaturally pale skin under his black hair, Dr. Molinero very much liked to be the center of attention and the lead scientist. "Did you get a chance to look at that work?"

"Of course, I have it right here." *ADAM, take it away.* She began to speak as the words vibrated into her earpiece. "To be honest with you, I have several concerns about your intern."

Intern? ADAM, what are you talking about?

Dr. Molinero frowned. "My intern?"

ADAM, you better have a good answer for this.

>>**Just keep saying what I tell you**<<

"I assumed this was an intern's work." Jennifer, realizing where ADAM was going with this, struggled to hold in her laughter. It was all she could do to frown in concern. "There are numerous very basic mistakes on the first few pages alone."

Dr. Molinero looked torn between anger and shame. "Dr. Yordan, this is not your area of expertise."

"It's not the area I've chosen to work in," Jennifer replied loftily, trying to add a theatrical flair to ADAM's suggestions, "but I happen to be well-versed in immunology. Not to mention, one doesn't have to know immunology to see that these calculations are off."

Dr. Molinero's face went even paler. "I do not appreciate the suggestion that something is wrong with my work."

"And *I* don't appreciate that when Mr. Marcari comes to check on our process, he's going to find that we were held up by incompetence this basic." Jennifer dropped the papers back on the desk.

"I was...just testing you!" Molinero's voice sounded wild.

She didn't need ADAM's expertise to know a lie when she heard one. "I know you were trying to test me. I also know this was your real work." She picked up the papers and held them out to him. "Consider this your warning, doctor. I won't go to Hugo, *this* time. But I will go to him if I ever see these sorts of mistakes in your work again."

She broke off as she saw Hsu walk by in the hallway. Immediately upon arriving, Jennifer had been taken to Hugo and Hsu had been bundled off in another direction, and Jennifer still needed to confer with the other woman.

Molinero saw her look. "What?"

"That...other new scientist. Which lab is she in?"

"Why?" He looked suspicious now.

Shit. Um...

"Because I haven't had a chance to inspect *her* work yet." Jennifer lifted her nose and swept out of the room.

5

Catalonia, Spain

One of the guards set a cup of coffee down at Gerard's side. "Anything else, sir?"

Gerard looked him over. The man's slightly rumpled uniform said DOMINGUEZ on the nametag. If Gerard remembered correctly, this man had come back from somewhere in Italy to serve Hugo. He'd been tanned and thin when he returned, but he'd been putting on weight. Gerard's lip curled. Dominguez would be useless in a fight.

He needed to institute a better training regimen, clearly.

"Nothing else," he replied shortly. "Leave me. And I am not to be disturbed, is that clear?"

"Yes, sir." Jacobo Dominguez left with his head down. He didn't want Gerard to see the flash of anger in his eyes.

The man would surely take offense, and Jacobo told himself that this was a good job. He could still see Gerard's eyes lingering on the wrinkles at the cuffs and collar, and so he straightened his uniform as he walked through the halls.

Not for the first time, Jacobo thought of quitting. He could keep telling himself all day long that the pay was good and the work was easy, but there had come a shift in the air.

The boss made surprise inspections of the facilities. New scientists were brought in and the old ones disappeared but —as Telmo pointed out—they never took their passports out of the safe in the guard captain's office. Gerard was everywhere, inspecting everything, and the experiments... The experiments had started to make Jacobo sad.

At first, he told himself that they were clearly criminals, sold from some of the local prisons. He heard about that sort of thing happening.

They'd been turned into actual *werewolves*, which was incredible. He wished he could tell people, but he could only talk about it with the other guards. The experiments were actually able to transform, just like in the books Jacobo read sometimes, and the scientists could make them attack targets who were probably other prisoners.

But even knowing they were prisoners, it had become upsetting to see them in their cages. They looked too thin and hopeless, even when they were wolves. Jacobo didn't like that.

He stopped as he caught sight of the new scientist through one of the windows. She was kneeling to whisper into one of the cages.

Maybe she felt sorry for the wolves, too.

Jacobo watched as she poked her fingers through the

bars. He would never have been brave enough to do that, but the wolf didn't bite them off like he feared might happen. Instead, she smiled and seemed to be scratching the wolf's muzzle.

Jacobo decided she was probably not the sort of person who would like Gerard, no matter that Gerard seemed to want her.

He also decided that if she was brave enough to put her fingers through the bars like that, then he was brave enough to say hello to her the next time he saw her.

Rules be damned.

Back in the guard captain's study, Gerard flipped through video clips of the new scientists.

So far, nothing looked incriminating.

He frowned and crossed his arms as he watched a clip of the dark-haired one. She spread the documents out on the table and looked them over, and then she looked up at the ceiling. He could see her lips moving.

Maybe she was doing calculations in her head? It would be strange, but scientists *were* strange.

Anyway, at least she wasn't taking pictures of the documents.

More video clips. She was well-behaved. She didn't talk much with the other scientists, as he'd been afraid she might. She didn't seem to like Molinero, which Gerard could understand. The man was a self-important ass who kept failing to get results.

Maybe she really was on the level. Maybe her story about joining the Velingrad facility was accurate.

Maybe it was the other one who was the traitor, the Chinese woman from Sofia. She'd been a captive there for eleven years without any escape attempts, but perhaps she had been a sleeper agent the whole time.

Gerard scanned the videos of her next. Like the other woman, Hsu was meticulous in her work. She filed papers neatly, she never took photos, and she seemed to avoid the other scientists whenever possible.

She did, however, seem strangely reluctant to perform experiments. For someone who claimed that this was her life's work, she always looked very unhappy

But the next video clip was very, very interesting: the two of them in close-headed conversation in one of the corridors.

Gerard's face broke into a smile. *At last.*

He watched while the two scientists conferred, and then he backtracked, slowed it down and watched the video again. They stood close together, but he did not see any flash drives or papers change hands.

But as they walked away from each other, Hsu looked nervously back over her shoulder as if to make sure no one was watching.

Gerard scanned the rest of the videos. None of them seemed to show anything wrong. The two women did not cross paths again. Neither of them sent messages to the other over the in-house servers, and there were no unauthorized attempts to contact the outside world via email. His elation was turning to frustration. If there was a nefarious purpose to them being here, he could not find it.

Still, he was sure something was wrong.

He stood up and left the room, walking quickly through the hallways. He barely noticed people flattened themselves against the walls to get out of his way, or that they watched him to see where he might go. They always liked to scurry in the other direction, like mice.

Like he couldn't find them.

He stopped in front of a lab. Gerard had suggested the windows on each lab. He didn't want the scientists to think they could shut themselves in and do whatever they wanted.

The dark-haired scientist, "Irina," was kneeling on the floor by one of the cages, stroking the muzzle of one of the wolves. She murmured something and stood, dusting off her hands.

She caught sight of him, and the smile vanished from her face.

Gerard turned and left wordlessly. Let her know she was being watched. Let her be afraid.

But she hadn't *seemed* afraid. She'd seemed to be daring him to make something of what he'd seen.

He didn't like that, and he'd show her as much, but not in the way she expected. He lifted a finger to flag down one of the guards.

"Find Ying Hsu and have her brought to the main house. Make sure she is walked past Laboratory 7."

The real problem was that all of this was boring as hell.

Jennifer stared at the paperwork spread out in front of her and waited for ADAM to say something.

Anything.

Literally anything.

She spent her days staring at paperwork, noting down changes and data as ADAM directed her to, and trying to appear aloof enough that the other scientists wouldn't bother her. Dr. Molinero was afraid of her since she had corrected his work, so he never came into her lab.

That was good. She hated him.

But she was lonely. In every mission prior, she'd had the camaraderie of her pack—and, later, her adopted pack and their allies. It made a difference to go into battle knowing there were people with you who had your back without question, people you would protect with your life. The jokes to take away the grimness of the fight, the encouragement to keep fighting when it seemed hopeless, and the reminder of *why* you were fighting.

She missed it.

She missed *Stephen*.

Alone in the lab, Jennifer squeezed her eyes shut and tried to keep the tears from escaping. She knew that ADAM could probably arrange for her to speak to Stephen, and the possibility had tormented her for two weeks. She hadn't been brave enough to ask, though—and Stephen hadn't tried, either.

He was probably furious.

How was she ever going to be able to explain to him that this was something she had to do? That she couldn't miss the opportunity to get the information they needed and still live with herself?

Because at the end of the day that was what it came down to.

Whether she decided to leave Earth with her new family, or stay with everything she had ever known, she was going to have to live with the choices she made.

Only by following her sense of honor, and pushing herself to the breaking point and beyond, could she find out where her heart lay—stay, and give up Stephen and her new family, or leave and give up the planet that had raised her, not knowing if she would ever come back.

She pressed her fingers against her eyes and counted to ten.

>>**Jennifer, are you okay?**<<

Let honor be your guide.

"I'm all right, yes. Thank you, ADAM." She picked her head up and swallowed. "Is the rest of the team on their way?"

>>**Yes. They are currently making a plan. Because of you, they know for sure where to target.**<<

"Good." She could hold out as long as was necessary...just as long as she knew her gamble was paying off.

She was shuffling through the papers again, however, when six guards marched by.

And between them was Hsu, hands cuffed in front of her.

Brussels, Belgium

Lance made his way around crates of engineering gear and into the sunny kitchen of the rental apartment. Located in a less-fashionable part of town, the old building was laced with so much metal that it was essentially a Faraday cage, so no smartphone-addicted youths wanted to rent it.

The apartment had been rented through three different cutouts and was theirs for the next six months. They hoped to be gone within the week, but hotels and short rentals tended to garner more scrutiny.

It was ideal for their purposes. Bobcat, Marcus, and William had spread their work out in the vaulted living room and were testing the tracker-blocking discs they'd developed for the shipping containers of Bethany Anne's shoes. There was a great deal of grumbling about impossibilities and doing all of this for shoes, but Lance had known enough engineers in his time to recognize the glint in their eyes.

They were enjoying the hell out of this.

His amused smile at the engineers faded as he observed the clipped conversation taking place in the kitchen.

Nathan had insisted on coming back to Earth, and there was still a definite chill in the air between him and Stephen. Neither had let the matter escalate even to raised voices because neither of them was foolhardy enough to risk another lecture from Bethany Anne.

The second lecture tended to be considerably less gentle than the first.

Still, even if their manners were polite, they were clearly angry with one another as they studied a map together. Stephen was leaning back in a chair, chin propped on one fist as he examined the topographical map, and Nathan's arms were crossed over his chest.

"You'll want to circle around and approach from the south," Nathan explained. "Ideally from the sea."

"I know," Stephen replied coldly. He looked at Nathan. "I thought you were planning another visit to Bulgaria?"

Nathan went to pour himself a cup of coffee. "There's not much to plan. Stoyan and Irina will take us to their former Alpha." He nodded to the corner, where the two Wechselbalg were deep in conversation with Peter.

Nathan was annoyed. His plan to speak to the Alpha of Stoyan's pack would not likely bring results. He had yet to meet a pack leader willing to give up their life and lead their pack entirely into the unknown, and very few even offered their pack the sanctioned chance to join Bethany Anne.

In all honesty, Nathan was not sure why he kept trying. Maybe it was just that he liked to believe the best of people. He wanted the packs both to understand that there was a place for them in the world Bethany Anne was building—a place where they did not have to hide—and to realize that the world beyond Earth was something that was also their concern.

The further you got from your old life on Earth, the more you realized just how petty the rivalries were.

None of them were going to survive long if something unfriendly came through that gate and decided to take Earth.

So far, his attempts to explain the danger to people weren't met with much success. He also didn't like the idea of Jennifer being alone in Spain, and Stephen going alone to scout out the rescue plan. Stephen was the one who had lost her in the first place.

"ADAM suggests Stephen disguise himself as a tourist." Lance couldn't see inside Nathan's head, but he could see the frustration well enough. "Catalonia has a number of historical tours that might point out possible castles to examine, and while Hugo doubtless has people in place to warn him about new people in town, we don't think he's watching the tour buses."

"A tourist." Stephen looked pained.

"You won't be alone, though." Lance grinned. "Guess who's going with you?"

Stephen stared at him. He could not imagine. Then he looked sharply over his shoulder into the other room, where a shout was closely followed by the sound of a small explosion.

"Them?" He gaped at Lance. "You think I'll be able to keep a low profile with *them*?"

Lance grinned. "A low profile? No. But you really think anyone's going to peg those three as geniuses unless they get near a set of wrenches? Besides, they need to scan the area for good evac routes for the shoes."

William stuck his head around the door. "I'm looking forward to seeing Spain. We aren't leaving until tomorrow, though, right?"

Lance gave him a look of deep misgiving. "Yes. Why?"

"Well, since we're in *Belgium*..."

Nathan, Stephen, and Lance only stared blankly until Bobcat pushed William aside.

"Beer," he explained. "Now come on. You guys want to sample the local culture, or what?"

. . .

Catalonia, Spain

Jennifer paced back and forth. In the fifteen minutes since Hsu had been marched past her office, she had come up with about a hundred plans to rescue the other woman —but none of them were exactly viable. "I have to help her," she muttered. She'd been saying that for the past few minutes, as if the urgency would help.

>>It is too dangerous to interfere.<<

She snapped, "You *think* I don't know that?" ADAM's calm voice had helped her sometimes when she felt out of her depth, but right now it annoyed her.

>>I simply fail to see how you can help her without interfering directly.<<

"So, what? I should just let her be executed?" Jennifer shot a look of pure fury up at the sky. "She's an ally. You don't just let an ally be hurt."

>>Perhaps they do not mean to hurt her.<<

"Then why would she be in cuffs?"

>>Many reasons. Perhaps she engaged in criminal conduct, and they are bringing her to a local police station. Perhaps, and more likely, they are wondering what you will do.<<

Jennifer sat down on her work stool with a thump. "Wait. You think that's why they're doing this?"

>>I only said it was possible. However, you have said that you think Gerard has doubts about you. Your cover stories state that you and Hsu both miraculously escaped the carnage at Velingrad. It is highly possible that he realizes you are connected, even if he does not know how.<<

"Oh, God," Jennifer whispered. "You mean I put her in danger by coming here?"

>>**Not necessarily. Hsu was abducted, remember. It would have taken us significantly longer to find her and rescue her without you coming here so that we could track you.**<<

"That's true." Jennifer bit her lip. "I just… I don't know what to do. Letting her face them alone seems wrong, doesn't it?"

There was a long pause.

"ADAM? Please say something."

>>**You must weigh the cost of losing against the benefit you can do if your cover is not compromised.**<< ADAM replied finally.

In reality, he did not want to say anything at all. Stephen's anger when he thought ADAM had encouraged Jennifer had given a new dimension to ADAM's calculations.

Now when he spoke, he was very aware that he was not only providing information but also influencing Jennifer toward a course of action. Which course was the least dangerous?

And, was that supposed to be his primary concern?

The more time he spent alive, the more he both enjoyed the world and found it a hopeless frustration. Bethany Anne's assurance that most humans were confused most of the time did not help in the slightest. It simply made the world a more terrifying place.

ADAM said nothing more now.

He did not trust himself to say the 'correct' thing. He simply watched as Jennifer rocked back and forth while she tried to decide. He wondered what choice she would make.

He wondered if it would be the correct choice. He wondered how he would know if it was.

———

Hsu shook with fear as she was brought through the hallways of the castle. Everything here smelled of decay and mildew; this was a place long past its prime.

But there was still a malevolent strength here, one she would not disregard. She had learned long ago that even if someone was not worthy of respect, they could still hurt you.

It was one of many reasons she had chosen not to go home again.

They brought her into an entirely bare room and guarded the door. There was nowhere to sit, and they did not tell her how long she was going to have to wait—or for whom she was waiting.

She knew how to deal with that. How to prevent the anxiety that was festering in her mind to grow, as was their plan. But it was one thing to know it and another to do it. Hsu tried to remember her training from years ago, the rules and advice for surviving an interrogation. In times of solitude, when one was left to fear what was coming next, they were instructed to focus on something physical nearby, and think of that and only that.

She fixed her eyes on the window that led out into the world and allowed everything else to fade from her mind.

There was sunlight.

There was the faint ripple in the old glass. She tried to imagine how the old curtains must once have looked, back when the castle was so fresh that the stone still smelled of the quarries.

Just the window. Nothing else. She tried to forget herself entirely, and did not move her hands lest the pull of the handcuffs remind her of her situation.

The door opened. Hsu closed her eyes for a moment to remind herself of the part she was playing. Then she opened her eyes again and turned to look at the two men who came into the room. Hugo looked annoyed, and Gerard looked truly angry.

"Sir." Hsu directed a small bow at Hugo.

"How is your research?" he asked her abruptly.

"Very good, sir." Hsu smiled as if she were genuinely pleased. "I've begun compiling all three facilities' results and am beginning to see trends in how quickly different techniques result in a form change and in obedience."

"What factors are you testing?" The question was sharp and quick, from Gerard this time.

"Everything I can," Hsu told him simply. "The duration in the facility, the size of both wolf and human, the approximate age of the subject and whether the prisoner was brought in from that same region. I am even noting the gender and age of the scientist."

Gerard was furious, "And you do not think this is a waste of Mr. Marcari's time?" Gender? Size of wolf? As far as he was concerned, this woman was a fraud. She should have been executed at Sofia.

He was also angry about the other scientist. The guards assured him that Dr. Irina Yordan had seen Hsu marched out of the facility, but after waiting for two hours for her interfere, it had become clear that she was not planning to rescue Hsu.

Which would mean that as far as Gerard could tell, he'd been wrong.

He hated being wrong.

"With all due respect, sir, the fact that we are still having this problem means that we have not yet determined its cause. It is necessary to step back and make use of the information that is before our eyes. Any difference, however small or strange it may seem, could be the key to unlock this for us."

"And you are seeing differences?" Hugo asked. He did not look at Gerard, who was quietly seething. He looked at the Chinese woman with the grey in her hair, who looked earnest and thoughtful.

"Some. One researcher at Velingrad was very successful." She looked down demurely. "I have also been very successful. I am seeing if I can compare the two videos to find any similarities, and will then cross-reference them against the unusually good times from every other researcher. Perhaps they sometimes do things differently without realizing—the tone of their voice, slightly different timings than expected. Anything."

"Good work." Hugo looked at Gerard. "I think we're done here."

He left immediately, and Hsu forced herself to keep smiling after him, but her smile faded when she saw the look on Gerard's face.

"Let's get one thing straight," he told her. His tone was not angry, it was almost happy. "Hugo does not like to be betrayed. He may trust you right now, but I know there's something off about you. I'll find out what it is, believe me." He gestured to the guards. "Take her back to the labs."

He stared after the woman as she left. She was nothing more than a good actress, he was convinced of that.

It hadn't worked to make the other doctor come after her. He would just need to try something different next time. Still, he was as curious as Hugo—who, exactly, had been poking around in the abandoned facility?

6

Sofia, Bulgaria

Irina strode through the outskirts of Sofia with Nathan, Peter, and Stoyan. Though the day was pleasant, with just the first touches of spring in the air, none of them spoke. Even in Europe, Irina had heard tales of Nathan. The American seemed to live up to the tales, with a look about him that said you didn't want to cross him. He apparently had the same prickly sense of honor that Stephen had, as well. Irina suspected that part of the reason the two were still so angry was that they were too alike—neither of them would back down. She knew better than to voice that aloud, though.

With the men silent, Irina became lost in her thoughts again and struggled to not run away. At the facility, in the rush of the escape, seeing Stoyan had been the best moment of her life. They had always been so alike. The fact that her family had come—not to save her, but to continue the work she started—had buoyed her up and given her the strength to keep fighting. Now that she was going back to her pack, she wasn't sure what to think. She hadn't wanted to come back at all, truth be told. But she knew that her experience inside the labs might tilt the scales. She hadn't even suggested not coming.

Not when she might make the difference between another pack getting saved, or not.

She could still feel what they had done to her, though— in her body, and in her mind.

Would that ever be over?

As if he had read her mind, Stoyan looked at her. "You don't have to come, you know." He kept his voice low, speaking with as much of an accent as he could to make the words indistinct to the others in their group.

"You know I have to." Irina did not look at him. He was pitying her, and she hated pity.

"No." He stopped and pulled her back to face him. "I love you, Irina. We're like twins, no?"

"We are." They'd been called that when they were little, and they'd always known what the other was thinking at a glance.

Now, she didn't *want* to know what he was thinking.

"I know you better than I know anyone else in this world," he continued seriously, "and I have to tell you, Irina, sometimes you are stubborn as a pig, and sometimes you can be very forgetful."

Her eyes narrowed. "What? What does that even mean?"

"You forget you have a pack. You went to Sofia alone rather than even *ask* for my help." He waved a hand to stave off her protest. "I know why you did it. And now you're determined to go because you want to tell them what happened. Well, I saw the labs. I spoke to some of the others. I could tell them what happened, and you wouldn't have to relive it."

Irina frowned. "I hadn't thought of that."

"Like I said, you can be very forgetful. I am here to help you, because you are my family and my friend. I will help you if you will allow it."

Irina reached out to take his hand. The skin on her hand was unblemished; she had healed quickly enough that there was now no trace of the burns and cuts she had suffered.

She still knew they had been there, though. It was as if she didn't trust her own eyes.

"You *are* helping me," she told him. "You came to get me out of there. You and I are working together to help the rest of them. And when we speak to the pack, you will be there at my side. That will help."

A thought occurred to her. "What do *you* want?"

"To free the rest of the packs in those facilities," he answered immediately.

"No—for everything." She struggled to explain it, "For your life."

His expression gave him away. He always seemed to have the same look when he thought of Arisha and Irina gave a sudden burst of laughter. She bit it off hastily when he glared and blushed.

"Is everything all right?" Nathan looked at them.

"I just, ah, swallowed wrong." Irina pretended to cough. "I'm fine."

"Well, if you're all right," he replied, "we should keep moving."

Stoyan and Irina went first through the underbrush as the moon rose overhead. They didn't talk, but they also didn't need to in order to communicate. Untroubled by the cold, and not yet tired by their hours of walking, they were beginning to relax as they got closer and closer to home.

Nathan and Peter hung back. After so much time working together, they didn't need to speak, either.

Peter smiled as he remembered the meeting during which he'd come to serve Bethany Anne. If you had asked him that day, he would have said that he hated everything she stood for, and saw no reason to follow her.

Nathan had set him straight. Peter had no doubt he could do the same here.

All four of them heard the rustle in the trees just before the attack hit. Nathan swung around, dropping toward the ground instinctively as his gaze scanned the trees. A snarling wolf shot overhead, skidded heavily on the leaves, and whipped around.

He could hear two more behind them. He and Peter would take those, and leave the ones in front to Stoyan and Irina unless they called for help.

As the wolf readied itself to spring once more, Nathan transformed. He leapt to meet the wolf in midair and the two clashed and fell with a snarl. They tumbled over and over, claws scrabbling for purchase, teeth seeking a throat.

This was a territorial dispute, and it was rare that any pack would begin with lethal force. These wolves were testing the group of intruders, and the only way for the intruders to win was to establish dominance so quickly that the border guards would not try to fight further.

Nathan's teeth found his opponent's throat and he was

able to press the other wolf down onto the ground. He bore down, snarling, until he heard the yip of surrender.

Peter, meanwhile, faced off with two of the others. He circled, always to the outside to keep the two wolves lined up—that way, only one of them could attack him at a time. As the first one darted in, going for his forelegs, the second leapt over them both to attack him from the other side.

Irina dashed in and collided with the first one. The two tumbled over one another and she snapped at his prone form with a snarl—*Back off.*

She transformed back. "So you had standing orders to attack us on sight?"

The wolf at her feet transformed with a cough of pain. He looked up at her with thinly concealed dislike.

"You're not our pack." He spat, "You're trespassing."

"She *is* your pack." Stoyan looked furious. He hadn't transformed, and two long scratches ran down the outside of one arm, healing even as he talked. "She disobeyed orders and left. But she's family, and she left in a way that did you no harm. You owe her more than this."

"And what about you?" the man challenged. He stood up and sneered as he looked Stoyan up and down. "Big man, went off to Sofia to fight the humans and now you think you're something special? You're nothing. You have no respect."

"*Enough.*" Nathan spoke quietly, but there was an unmistakable command in his voice.

Everyone in the clearing fell silent.

Nathan looked at the attacker. "You will take us to your Alpha, and you will be silent while you do so."

"Why should I listen to you?" the man challenged.

He stumbled back as Nathan's hand closed around the front of his throat.

"Because I serve a Queen more powerful than you could ever dream," Nathan replied softly. "And the offer I make you tonight could be the difference between your pack's salvation and its destruction. Could be...depending on what you decide. Based on what I've seen so far?" Nathan squinted, "I don't have high hopes."

Brussels, Belgium

Bobcat, William, and Marcus lay with their heads on the cool marble of the countertop. A groan made its way around the room, and each of them had their eyes closed tightly against the morning light.

"Too bright," Marcus managed. "Why so bright?"

"Judgment of the gods," William croaked.

Bobcat only made a slightly pained noise of agreement. His vaunted ability to handle a quantity of beer no mere mortal could stand had been sorely tested.

He'd taken the last beer out of the refrigerator but had decided to use it as an ice pack instead of a beverage. He wasn't sure he could stomach the idea of more beer before he'd had a proper breakfast.

"Good morning." Stephen opened the door and came in with a box of pastries.

"Not so loud," William protested.

"Mercy," Marcus added. "Please, *mercy*."

"No time for that. We're leaving in two hours." Stephen set the box of pastries down on the table and gave them all a look. "I suggest coffee and pastries. That, and a good plan for the shoes."

Bobcat waved the beer bottle without picking his head up. "We made one."

"Last night? After drinking half of Belgium?" Stephen asked, disbelief coloring his voice.

"'S a good plan, I promise." Bobcat waved the beer vaguely. "'S on the table."

Stephen raised an eyebrow as he looked over the diagrams. He began to laugh, causing moans of complaint from the others, but he couldn't stop.

"I'll be damned." He looked over the plans a second time, and a third. "You all made a military-grade extraction arrangement while drunk off your asses. From now on, I'll make sure to have beer on hand when you engineer things."

"I like that plan," William agreed wistfully.

Stephen pulled together the notes, "But right now, you have to get up and moving."

William croaked back, "Oh, I don't like that plan."

Catalonia, Spain

Hsu walked through the corridors, still trembling with nerves. Initially, her mind had been blank with terror, but now she was beginning to see a pattern.

She had to play Hugo and Gerard off one another.

It wasn't going to be easy. She only had Gerard to work with, for one thing. Hugo rarely inspected the labs, and almost never called people up to the main house.

Maybe she could manufacture a reason.

A hand shot out from one of the side hallways and clamped down over Hsu's mouth before she could scream. Hsu found herself wedged into a tiny alcove, scant inches from her captor.

"It's just me," the new scientist called. "It's okay."

Hsu sagged with relief. "Thank god. We're not being watched here, I take it?"

"No. I got a look at the security feeds, and there's no camera that can see this angle."

"Then we'd better hope no one was watching me, and expecting me to show up on another camera."

"Eventually, we're going to have to take some risks." Jennifer was vaguely annoyed by the other woman's cool manner. "Are you all right?"

"Yes. For now. Gerard thought he would call me up to the house for Hugo to ask questions, but I'm still not sure why." Hsu shook her head. "They didn't really ask me anything. They just left me in a room for a long time."

"Oh, no." Jennifer sighed. "I was afraid of this. They're using you to get to me."

"Ah. Yes. On that point...who *are* you?" Hsu lifted a brow. "All you said the other day was to be brave and that there was backup coming, but who are you? You're not Irina."

"My name is Jennifer. I came here because we needed to find Hugo's headquarters. There are people coming here to help."

"What people?" Hsu questioned. Americans, in her experience, tended to be *very* unfocused in their discussion.

"TQB," Jennifer replied simply.

Hsu's eyes got wide. She'd heard of TQB in whispers, but all she really knew was that Hugo hated them, and she wasn't even sure why that was.

"Is that a rival company? Is that why Hugo hates you?"

"No, and no." Jennifer was trying to find the words to explain when they heard the tread of the patrols. "Go. I'll make sure you get out with us when they get here. It won't be long. Be brave, and if they try to use me to make you do something, don't give in, okay?"

And she was gone. Hsu stared after her.

Did she dare hope for rescue?

Or should she wait until this woman, this ally, was gone with the experiments—and then take Hugo and Gerard out?

Jennifer half-ran through the hallways back to her lab. Her heart was pounding with relief.

They'd bought themselves a bit more time.

In the lab, she did a quick round to see how the Wechselbalg were doing. Some came to sniff her fingers, others —in human form—nodded to her, but many were still too scared to trust her, even with the smell she carried.

Those broke her heart.

She sat on the floor in the corner of the lab, not visible from the window at the front, and considered.

And then she did the thing she'd been terrified to do.

"ADAM? Can you get me in touch with Stephen?"

There was a pause. Then, >>**Yes, of course. One moment.**<<

The next pause seemed so long that she could swear she was going to go out of her mind with worry.

"*Jennifer?*" Stephen's voice was tight with worry.

Jennifer pressed a hand over her mouth and tried not to let the sob out. It took two deep breaths before she could speak. "Hi."

"*What's wrong?*"

"Nothing's wrong." She clenched her hands together. "But I miss you, and I'm sorry about what I did."

She thought she heard him sigh slightly, and her heart fell. Sometimes she felt very young compared to Stephen.

"I understand why you did it," he said at last.

"What? Really?" She hadn't expected that.

"It was pointed out to me, by a certain queen we know, that you did exactly what I would have done if I thought I had the opportunity."

Jennifer gave a watery laugh.

"She reminded me of what you are," Stephen said.

"And what is that?"

"A warrior, and a fine one. One of her best. A woman who won't let danger stand in her way." Stephen paused. "Please tell me you're safe."

"About as safe as I'd be getting into shenanigans with you," Jennifer pointed out.

Stephen laughed. The sound was genuine, full-throated, and Jennifer leaned her head back against the wall, smiling as tears leaked out of her eyes. She'd missed him.

"You're not angry?"

"Not anymore. You gave us the final key to nail this guy. And we'll see each other soon, won't we?"

"Yeah, we will." Jennifer smiled. "And in the meantime,

I'm doing as much as I can to get their research moving backward. ADAM's been invaluable. I'm just trying to see if there's any way I can get into the rest of their servers so I can screw up everyone else's results, too."

"We'll see what we can manage." Stephen sounded amused. "Or we could just shoot them in the face."

Jennifer tapped her lips twice, "The hell with my plan, let's go with that."

"Just promise me one thing."

"Sure."

Stephen hesitated a moment. "The next time you jump into the unknown like that? Take me with you. It's killing me not to be fighting my way out of there with you."

"It's killing me, too." Jennifer's lips twitched into a smile. "I promise. I'll see you soon—and then we'll never do this sort of thing again."

"Deal," Stephen agreed emphatically.

7

Catalonia, Spain

"Arisha, right?" Gerard's voice was as smooth and pleasant as she remembered. He strolled closer, hands in his pockets.

Arisha froze. She told herself to keep breathing. Gerard knew nothing, she told herself fiercely. She was sure he hadn't seen her at Velingrad.

He knew nothing.

She smiled, as brilliantly as she could, as if she were delighted to see him. She made her accent strong and turned his name into a question. "Gerard? You are from here?"

"Didn't you know that already, my dear?"

There was a definite threat in his eyes. Arisha shook her head. "We never got our dinner, remember?" Her mind raced. How would she normally react if a man didn't call her? She settled for arching an eyebrow. "Did you find more charming company in Sofia, then?"

Gerard paused, his brow furrowing. He had seen her at

Velingrad…hadn't he? He had seen her on the security feeds. He was sure of it.

"Neither of us stayed in Sofia that night," he said simply.

"*You* did," Arisha pressed. "I saw you in the hotel, coming back around eleven." She crossed her arms. "What else am I to think, but you found a better way to spend your night? Or do you have so many women that you cannot remember where you were?"

She was walking a delicate line here, she knew. Getting information out of Gerard would mean that she had to pretend she hadn't been at Velingrad, and that she was disappointed not to have spent the night with him. But if she was too petulant, he would hardly want to spend time with her now.

She gave a nervous laugh and looked away. "I am sorry. It is not my place to be upset with you."

Silence. She did not dare to sneak a glance.

"In fact, I know it is not my place to ask anything of you." She looked up to meet his eyes at last and tried not to shiver at how cold they were. "But if this is, indeed, where you live, perhaps you could let me know which places might be best for a tourist. What should they see while they are here?"

"What?" Gerard was thrown off by this question.

"I write travel articles," Arisha explained. "Do you not remem— Never mind. If there is anywhere you would recommend, I would love to try it."

"I thought you wrote travel articles about how terrible it was in the Eastern Bloc after countries left the Soviet Union." Gerard was testing her now. "How did you like Velingrad?" He laid the trap smoothly.

He had to swallow his anger when she opened her eyes wide. "Sir, I see now why you are confused. We met in *Sofia*." She lifted a shoulder. "I quite liked Sofia, really. It was charming, did you not think so? But I had to write a bad article anyway. I begged my editor. I said, 'if you only send me to bad places, people will think this is not really a travel column.' He finally agreed to send me somewhere I could say was nice. Like this." She let her smile fade slightly. "You probably think I am...stalking? I do not mean you to think I chase you. I will go."

"No." His hand closed around her arm like a vise.

To scream, or not to scream? Arisha looked at him and saw him force a charming smile. The effect was terrifying.

"Let me show you around tonight," Gerard suggested. "I promise I won't stand you up again."

Despite the fact that she knew she should see if she could create a weak link in Hugo's defenses, or see if she could learn something useful, there was only one instinct in her head: *get out!* Arisha stammered, "You don't...you don't need to—"

"I insist."

"I, ah...let me get a coat." *And pray that someone sees me leave with him, so I don't vanish.*

"Tell me more about this proposal you have for me." Hugo strolled through the courtyard at the center of his castle. Diego Garza, a politician from Madrid, walked nervously beside him.

"You have spoken very strongly against TQB." Garza

began. "I am here to see if I cannot persuade you to change your mind."

Hugo glanced at the man. He wore an ill-fitting suit and seemed out of place amidst the opulence of the garden. Once, this had been a place of beaten earth, smelling of horses and hot metal from the forges. Now that battles were fought with computers and squads of elite soldiers he had ordered the courtyard be transformed as an homage to his family.

Statues of his forebears were surrounded by flowers, the meaning of which he had chosen carefully. His family's crest dotted the banners that fluttered around the walls.

Hugo could tell that this man was "self-made"—just a new way to say that he was a commoner who wanted to rise in the world.

From his nervousness, it was clear this commoner realized he was out of his depth.

Hugo's father would have had the man killed for coming into the family's estate and asking a lord to change his mind on an important matter. But Hugo liked to be magnanimous. He liked to give people a chance to change their minds before he exacted punishment.

"Why do you think I should change my position on this matter?"

The politician seemed surprised by Hugo's openness. "Ah, uh…."

Hugo only waited. He stopped before a statue of his great-grandfather and looked up at the man's stern face. This man had begun to see the world change, as industry emboldened the merchants and gave the commoners a false sense that they could have everything they wanted—even control of their own governments.

"Have you heard stories of the technology TQB wields?" the politician suggested finally.

"I have." Hugo did not look away from the statue.

"You know that this technology could aid the whole world with regards to medical science, astrophysics and space exploration, energy sources, communications." The man was fairly babbling with excitement. "This could be the next great leap in our world."

"Could it?" Hugo asked simply.

The man faltered in the face of his coldness. "Y-yes."

"Do you believe this, despite the fact that they have not shared this technology with us?"

"They do not yet trust us," the politician replied.

"And we cannot trust them. Mr. Garza, I am not a lone holdout against some utopian future. I am a skeptic for good reason. If TQB wanted to help the world, they have had ample opportunity to do so. Instead, we have reason to believe that they have undertaken numerous missions against sovereign governments, in defiance of international law."

"And we have evidence that those governments were conducting illegal research, *and* provoked those attacks," the politician argued. "There is also evidence that attacks on sovereign territory do not constitute attacks on those governments. It appears that rogue elements might be attempting to mimic TQB's technology for nefarious purposes."

Nefarious. Trust a commoner not to understand. Hugo smiled coldly. "Nefarious purposes such as…?"

"Attempts to seize power," the man explained. "Why, even within the governments themselves, different factions are trying to use this issue to seize power—with aspirations of global power."

"And you believe that…" Hugo looked at him, amused.

"That TQB seeks a united world," the politician argued. "The CEO's statements, though they are very few, seem to suggest that she does not trust the world with these technologies yet. If she thinks we are worthy of them, however, if we show that we are worthy of them—"

"So, if we bow and scrape in order to conform to her idea of 'honor.'" Hugo did not bother to disguise his contempt. "I think you will find very few allies if this is your course of action."

"It is not bowing and scraping!" The man drew himself up. "Our world has problems, Mr. Marcari, very severe problems. If we show that we are committed to fixing those problems, to building a world that can understand honor and responsibility, we will open the door to a future far greater than any we can imagine. That is not bowing and scraping, it is *rising*."

"You are a fool," Hugo told him simply. "You are a naïve fool who does not realize that TQB seeks to overturn the natural order of things. But there is only so much the world can take. The issue now is that the governments of Earth are too fractured within themselves to make any meaningful choices—and that problem is not only intrinsic to governments. It will solve itself."

"Mr. Marcari—"

"Get out of my house." Hugo did not look at him.

The man, to his credit, did not argue. But at the edge of the courtyard, he turned and looked back.

"You say you are not the lone holdout," he said defiantly. "But you will be. Others are listening. They understand what I say. All you do is rob the people of the world of what should be theirs—and I will not stop telling them to demand it."

He left with the air of a man who felt he had won an argument, and Hugo stared after him, chilled.

He could quite easily gain the loyalty of the governments, he was sure of that. Once the first few rebels had been put down like dogs, the rest would fall into line.

But a concerted uprising of the people, however doomed it might be against armies of shapeshifters, would be bloody. It would rob him of his workforce in huge numbers as he was forced to execute them, and it would give the governments an excuse to question him.

That he could not allow.

He took his phone out of his pocket and dialed a number. When the person on the other end answered, he did not bother with pleasantries. "The man who is leaving the castle. See to it that he does not make it back to Madrid. And get a story ready for the papers, that this man was assassinated by TQB."

The sound of huffing and puffing was harsh in the evening air as Bobcat, Marcus, and William scrambled up one of the hills beyond the town.

"You know what I like about the *Meredith Reynolds?*"

Marcus commented wistfully, his breath puffing. "All the floors are flat."

"Judging by how much you miss that, you could use the exercise." Stephen strode behind them with a grin, one eyebrow raised.

"I don't see why you had to come along," Marcus muttered. "You're not working on the shoes."

"For one thing, ADAM is presently working his way into the computer systems, which is something I cannot help with. For another, my distance vision is superb." Stephen looked at the other man. "Try breathing deeply. Panting won't help anything."

"How would you know? When was the last time you had trouble doing anything?"

"Several years ago, before I met Bethany Anne." Stephen looked amused. "I was, functionally speaking, about ninety years old. I could hardly walk."

"Then have some sympathy," William croaked.

"Part of your problem is that you're still hungover," Stephen explained. "Hydration is key, as I understand it."

"Uh-huh. I'll take that into consideration next time." Bobcat squinted across the valley then squatted, trying to get a line of sight into the hills. He pointed. "I'm thinking right there for the extraction. They shouldn't be able to see it from the castle."

"There isn't a road that leads there," Marcus protested.

"The ground is relatively flat. We'll just bribe some police officers to look the other way."

"You'd better use an intermediary," Stephen advised, "or they'll assume you're stupid foreigners, take the bribe, and then stop the truck, anyway." He shrugged at the expressions on their faces. "I'm happy to go away and take my advice with me, but I *do* know a fair amount about most European cultures. Centuries of experience will do that."

"Could *you* deliver the bribe?" Bobcat asked delicately.

"That's the first sensible suggestion you've made. Actually, I lie—that place looks very good for extraction. And yes, I will arrange the bribe." Stephen grinned. "It's been awhile since I got to do any fun accents."

"Right, well, that's settled." Bobcat waved to Marcus and William. "Come on, let's get back to the hotel."

"I'll meet you there in a bit," Stephen told them. "There's something I want to do before heading back."

Montpellier, France

Maurice awoke to the sound of his phone ringing insistently from the other side of the room. He swore as he stumbled through the semi-darkness.

"Maurice." Henri's voice was abrupt. "Are you with the truck?"

Those had been the instructions—stay with the truck at all times.

Maurice had taken one look at the tiny bunk in the back of the cab and decided he wanted nothing to do with that. Henri was crazy if he thought Maurice was *really* going to sit in a baking-hot truck for the next two days until someone got him a tire.

But Henri liked to say that things had to go 'by the book.'

"Yeah, I'm with the truck."

"Good. Someone's coming with a tire. You'll need to head out immediately."

"What?" Maurice cast about in a sudden panic. He held the phone with his ear as he hopped around on one foot, trying to put on his pants. "Tonight?"

"Of course, tonight. The client wants the truck in Catalonia by midday."

"Catalonia?" Son of a bitch. "I thought I was going to Madrid."

"Catalonia will be quicker, no? It's closer."

Maurice stared at the phone in pure hatred. Catalonia might be closer, but the remote villages of that region lay along tiny, winding roads, often unpaved. He was going to have to drive all night, taking no breaks, and staying alert while he did it.

He shook off the last of his sleep. "Fine. I'll start out in a few. I have to, ah...go pay the person who let me park. In case I'm not there when the guy arrives."

"I said not to leave the truck," Henri growled ominously.

"Then you should have arranged payment, shouldn't you? I can, ah...see it from here." He pulled on his shirt, still holding the phone with his ear, and tried not to make the floorboards creak as he made his way to the stairs. It had been a bitch and a half to get a room anywhere, and the one old woman who offered him her attic was so clingy. He couldn't afford to have her wake up. "Send a text with the town in Catalonia. I'll be back with the truck in three days."

"Make sure you get there by noon," Henri advised. "Or we don't get paid. And then I don't pay your petrol."

Maurice swore and hung up as he hurried down the stairs.

Who *were* these people? And what was in the damned truck that they needed so badly?

Only a sense of self-preservation stopped him from opening the truck to peek inside. If the police stopped them—which was seemingly more and more likely—it was best to know nothing.

8

Bulgaria

"Thank you for hearing me out." Nathan turned slowly as he spoke, to meet the eyes of every pack member. "I would take more time with this, but we do not have time. What we have is a problem that needs solving."

Karliman Zukanov crossed his arms and scowled. Since Irina and Stoyan left, the latter taking four strong fighters with him, Karliman's grip on the pack had been tenuous. Even with the false stories he'd put out, six members leaving was a sign that he could no longer maintain control of the pack.

He resented that. He'd done the only sensible thing to keep his packmates safe. Did they really think it was wise to throw themselves against a much stronger enemy? Did they think they could possibly win? He knew they could not. The best they could do was try to stay safe.

Every few decades, there was someone who tried to enslave the Wechselbalg. Every one of them tripped up and died.

They just had to wait, goddammit.

To be honest, he'd been hoping that word would reach them of their former packmates' gruesome deaths. That would illustrate his point nicely. He'd hoped for it right up until the moment they strode back into the camp, looking hardly the worse for wear, and with another Wechselbalg who made Karliman's hackles go up.

This man, this *Nathan*, had an aura about him that Karliman had tried to cultivate for years. He realized now that he had failed. Nathan was a man you did not want to cross, that much was clear. He had taken the attention of the pack without even raising his voice, and something about him made you pray that he never raised his voice.

"I am Nathan Lowell, originally from New York." Nathan folded his arms. "I will skip my personal history—what you need to know is that I now serve Queen Bethany Anne of TQB."

There was a murmur from the group. There had been rumors about TQB, but few in the pack had given any thought to them. With video surveillance and social media, governments were more of a concern for the Wechselbalg packs.

Anything that distracted the governments, therefore, was considered a bonus. The pack hadn't cared much about TQB beyond hoping they continued to be a thorn in the side of governments everywhere.

Nathan smiled grimly as he continued, "My Queen is more powerful than you can imagine. She is, as it seems few of you are aware, the Matriarch. She has taken Michael's place."

The camp went dead silent.

"Yes," Nathan continued quietly. "Now you see. You may be accustomed to Michael's brand of honor. Hers is different, but believe me when I say that it is just as uncompromising."

The pack looked wary now, and Nathan couldn't blame them. Michael's rigid sense of honor had been the stuff of legend.

He wondered what they would say about Bethany Anne.

"A few weeks ago, my Queen learned of the abductions of Wechselbalg families across Europe. She sent Stephen, her deputy in Europe, to investigate. By now, you may have heard what happened in Velingrad—the bulk of the Wechselbalg there were rescued. In Sofia, the Wechselbalg staged an uprising." Nathan hesitated. "Almost all of them were killed."

All eyes went to Irina, who was looking down at the ground.

She had feared this moment, but now that it was here, she found purpose in it. She looked around at her former pack mates and met Karliman's eyes and spoke.

"The man who runs these facilities is called Hugo Marcari," she told them, "and he wants to rule the world with us as his enforcers. In his facilities, we were tortured. They did anything they could to hurt us, to make us say that we would be his servants. They have developed techniques to force us to change forms and attack. They forced us to attack family who were not shifters. You see, Hugo abducted whole families because he knew that the ability was passed down."

They stared at her in horror.

"There are more facilities," Irina continued, "and Hugo is still alive. We need him *dead*. We need every one of those facilities shut down, and his allies dead as well. They have done things for which there can be no forgiveness. Stand with me, and we will make him pay for what he has done. Stand back, and you will know that you turned your face away from the slaughter of our kind."

Nathan could understand her passion, but he knew that Irina might be pushing too far, and too fast.

"We do not ask you to act alone," he told them. "My Queen has sent supplies and fighters. You would not be walking into this fight blind. In truth, we could take these facilities out on our own."

"Why aren't you?" Karliman challenged him.

Nathan smiled. The man had given him the perfect opening. "Because you have been wronged. Someone has taken your packmates and tortured them, forced them to kill. My Queen will not tolerate such things, but she also knows that she should not deny you your own justice, meted out by your own pack."

There was a long silence. Karliman was silent, and Nathan watched him closely. It was obvious to Nathan that the pack's Alpha had been hoping that Bethany Anne would be issuing orders. Orders that he could then contest. Nathan, instead, had portrayed the situation as an opportunity—and one the rest of the pack looked eager to take.

"We will talk about this alone," Karliman said abruptly. "You three, go to the overlook. I will join you there to tell you the pack's decision."

Stoyan tried not to flinch. The words were a reminder that he and Irina had given up their place in this pack. But it would do no good to protest. He nodded silently and followed Nathan and Irina from the grove.

Catalonia, Spain

Stephen's footsteps crunched slightly on the rocky path as he climbed toward the castle.

He shouldn't be here. It was a temptation he didn't need.

>>Stephen, do you need anything from me?<<

He should have known ADAM would be watching. Although, in the case of an AI, "watching" wasn't exactly accurate. It was simply difficult to do something without one noticing.

"No, ADAM. I just wanted to see the place before attacking it."

>>I can send you more blueprints.<<

Stephen smiled. "Are you worried? I won't be seen."

>>I am simply unsure why seeing the castle makes a difference.<<

Stephen crested the hill and knelt, so as not to catch the eye of any guards watching from the facility or the castle. The two buildings sat a scant distance apart, one up on the hill and traditionally defensible, the other at the outskirts of town, hidden by trees and walls.

His eyes lingered on the facility. Jennifer was there, and even knowing that he would see her in a day or so, Stephen still fought the urge to fight his way into the facility, kill anyone and everyone standing in his way, and get to her side.

Patience.

He remembered that ADAM had expressed confusion. "Think of it as a way of focusing emotions. While I wait for the attack, seeing this place reminds me of what I fight for."

>>Do you forget?<<

"No." Stephen smiled slightly. "It's difficult to explain. A sense of purpose in a battle can turn the tide, ADAM. I have seen it over the centuries countless times. When soldiers—"

He broke off and drew further into the shadows.

A group of guards climbed the hill from the town, singing drunkenly. Their uniforms had the logo of Hugo's operations, and they were oblivious to anything but their own enjoyment.

Stephen's anger rose until it choked him, and his hands curled into fists. These guards *knew* what happened in that facility, and they were returning willingly to their work at the castle. He wanted to appear from the darkness like their worst nightmare and fill them with terror before he tore them limb from limb.

Patience. He forced himself to stand still as they passed. None of them looked into the shadows to see the glint of his eyes—red, now, with his fury.

They would know his face tomorrow. He promised himself that.

The screech of tires sounded from somewhere in the valley and Stephen turned to look. There was no sound after that for a long moment.

And then a single gunshot echoed out.

Stephen started running.

．　．　．

QBBS Meredith Reynolds

"My Queen?"

Bethany Anne, presently in the middle of examining a new green space on the ship, noticed the note of worry in Stephen's voice immediately. "What is it? Is everyone alright?"

"All of our people, yes. But someone has been assassinated near Hugo's estate. I believe he was visiting before he was killed. I heard the gunshot."

"You're there now?"

"Yes, but I can't get closer. There are a lot of police already."

"That's odd, for somewhere so remote."

"Not really." There was anger growing in Stephen's voice. "They're from one of the bigger cities. They must already have been on their way when the assassination was carried out. They aren't upset, though, as if they had been trying to stop it and failed—so they may be in on it."

"Let me guess." Bethany Anne strode away into the trees, trying to keep her voice down so as not to alarm the children who were running through the undergrowth with delighted shrieks. "They've got someone in mind to blame for this."

"Yes," Stephen agreed simply. "From what I've heard, we've apparently released a statement taking responsibility for his death."

"That's fucking ridiculous. Why the hell would I execute one of Hugo's associates – and on the side of the road?"

>>I believe I may have the answer.<< ADAM chimed in. >>This man, Diego Garza, was a known moderate

and did not agree with EU policies that condemned you. It seems to be a pattern in human history that moderates are assassinated as a prelude to war, in an attempt to vilify the other side.<<

Bethany Anne managed a small smile. "Ah, ADAM, what would we do without you? I think you're correct. Someone is trying to frame us. The question is, is it the EU or someone else?"

"It could be anyone," Stephen said quietly. "Hugo had the easiest means—and so close to his castle, it could point to him. But he could also say he's being framed."

Bethany Anne closed her eyes. *I swear to god, if these scrotum-trailing, cum-wiping bastards think they're going to pin this on me, I am going to—*

No. She'd said she would stay out of it. *Son of a bitch.* Her patience was getting more frayed by the moment. "What are you going to do?"

"Kill him," Stephen said. "I'm not going to try sucking up to the media. That's a loser's game. I'm going to make sure justice gets that bastard, and then we're coming home."

Bethany Anne grinned. "That's the spirit. Good luck, and tell Jennifer I said hello."

"Will do."

On the *Meredith Reynolds,* Bethany Anne stared through the tiny forest with narrowed eyes.

"Retail therapy," she explained finally.

Are you actually going to wear all of these shoes? TOM questioned.

"TOM, it's either buy shoes or go back to Earth and do something—possibly involving firebombing."

Right. Shoes it is.

France

The phone buzzed on the seat next to him and Maurice gave it an annoyed look. He didn't want to talk to Henri.

But Henri, he knew from experience, would just keep calling.

"*Quoi?*"

"There will be two more trucks joining you," Henri told him. "Wait at the border until they arrive. Our client has extended the deadline to sundown."

Maurice hung up without saying a word. If they were extending the deadline, why had he had to get up and start driving now?

And what the hell was in these trucks?

Catalonia, Spain

"Sir?" A uniformed guard was waiting for Hugo at the door of the courtyard.

"What is it?" Hugo continued walking.

The guard fell in behind him. "I was looking over police reports and found one about a truck inbound to Spain. At the time, they did not specify where in Spain they were going, but a sizable sum was paid from a protected account to keep the police from looking inside the truck. Since then—"

Hugo turned to look at the guard.

The man's voice broke off. He swallowed and ducked his head.

"You've done well," Hugo told him finally.

"Sir?" The relief was palpable in the man's voice.

"Was there more?"

"Yes, sir. The truck appears to be waiting at the border. I'm not sure for what, but its destination on the crossing documents appear to have been edited." The man held out a piece of paper—a scan of a form. MADRID had been written in the location field, crossed out, and replaced with CATALONIA.

Hugo made sure to keep his face calm. In times of crisis, when anticipating attack, his father had told him that lesser men would panic and give in to anxiety. It was a lord's job to convince them that the defenses were equal to an attack and that each servant's talents were vital to the defense of the castle. Feeling as if they were valued and necessary increased loyalty.

"Thank you for bringing this information to me," Hugo continued gravely. "Dominguez, is it?"

"Yes, sir. Jacobo Dominguez."

"Good. I think you will rise in this organization, Dominguez. I want you to keep monitoring this personally. With this advance warning, we will have plenty of time to make sure that no unsavory elements are able to make their way into our town."

Jacobo ducked his head again. "Should I pass along any instructions to the guard captain, sir?"

"Yes. Tell him to call in reinforcements and alert Mr. Cordova that this has happened." Hugo's lip curled. Why had Gerard not been the one to bring him this information? He had not seen the man since that useless meeting with the scientist. "Furthermore, I expect regular updates on this situation. I expect them from *you*, Dominguez."

"Yes, sir." The man nodded with a renewed sense of purpose and hurried away to the guard barracks.

Hugo watched him go, frowning. He was certain of one thing: no one would deliver anything so secretive and important to this town unless it was damaging to him. There was no other purpose—no big factories, no other rich inhabitants.

Someone was moving against him at last. Was it TQB, or some other element in Europe?

When those trucks arrived, he meant to have them surrounded and seized.

For now, he would have to keep his eyes open. If these were weapons—and what else could they be?—then there would surely be mercenaries arriving as well. He picked up his phone.

"Message for Dominguez," he said shortly. "Tell him to watch the town as well. I want reports on anyone suspicious."

QBBS *Meredith Reynolds*

A ding sounded from the computer terminal, and Bethany Anne refreshed the page on her email, idly. She smiled when she saw the title:

Confirmation: Your Order Has Shipped

9

Catalonia, Spain

"You're *sure* it will be here by tomorrow evening?" The hooded figure kept his voice low. "We have a very tight timeframe for getting it out of here."

"It will be here in time, don't worry." The other man leaned forward into the shadows of the alleyway.

Pressed against the wall around the corner, Jacobo Dominguez struggled to hear the words. English, which almost certainly meant foreigners, and they were talking about a secret shipment.

He'd been looking for Gerard when he saw the two conspirators hurry into an alley. His heart was beating very fast now as he tried to spy on them. The darkness made him jump at every little sound, and he was afraid that if they came out and he couldn't hide, he would have to fight.

But he had to get this information. If someone was bringing weapons into the valley to assault the facility, it was imperative that Jacobo find out everything he could.

Only then could he make sure the facility and the castle were safe.

He thought of the new, brown-haired scientist. He didn't want anything bad to happen to her.

"And you'll get it across town?" the hooded figure asked urgently. "Remember, it has to be done with complete secrecy. None of the others can know."

Jacobo's eyebrows rose. Perhaps some of the weapons smugglers were planning to betray the others. That would thin their ranks before they could attack. That was good.

"No one will know," the other one assured him. "Seven crates, like we agreed. I'll deliver them whenever the road is clear."

"Good. I'll be in contact with payment."

As footsteps sounded, Jacobo squeezed himself into a doorway and prayed not to be seen. He only dared turn his head slightly as the two figures left the alley, one crossing immediately into another alleyway, and the hooded figure heading toward the center of town.

That was all he could do now—on his own. Jacobo waited until the street was empty, and then he pulled out his phone and dialed with shaking fingers.

"Mr. Marcari? It's Jacobo Dominguez. The crates will be delivered across town somewhere, and there might be some divisions we can exploit between the members."

William looked over as Bobcat came back into the apartment, "Where the hell were you?"

"I had to run out for a few." Bobcat pulled the hood off

his head and smiled. "Making sure everything was set for tomorrow."

"You didn't want us to come with you?" Marcus asked.

"You two were chilling out, no need to get you off the couch." Bobcat looked at the TV. "How the hell did you get NASCAR in the middle of Spain?"

"For an engineer," William stated loftily, "anything is possible."

"We repurposed some of the equipment we didn't need for the signal blockers," Marcus explained. "Want to watch?"

Bobcat frowned, "I was never much of a NASCAR guy...ah, hell, it's good to relax, right?" He chose a chair and kicked off his shoes. "Where's Lance?"

"Back on the *ArchAngel*. Says not to get into any trouble." Marcus tossed Bobcat a beer.

"Cool." Bobcat settled back in his chair and allowed himself a small, satisfied smile. As of tomorrow evening, he was going to be the owner of seven crates of very rare hops.

It was going to give him just the edge he needed in the competition.

Bulgaria

Nathan was nearing the end of his patience when Karliman came out of the forest behind them. He was accompanied by three other Wechselbalg—an older woman with greying hair and watchful eyes, a young man who looked like the stereotypical bodyguard, and a man who looked so much like Stoyan that Nathan did a double take.

Any hope that Nathan had, however, was dashed when he saw Karliman's eyes.

"The pack has voted," Karliman stated abruptly. "We will not intervene in this matter."

He seemed to be waiting for Nathan to bluster, so Nathan said nothing at all. He let the silence hang awkwardly, and he looked at Irina and Stoyan.

He wished he hadn't.

Stoyan looked utterly betrayed, and Irina looked like she was going to throw up.

"Why?" Irina asked. The one word shook.

"This man says his pack can defeat this Hugo Marcari on their own," Karliman replied contemptuously. "We aren't needed."

"What we *need* is to take action when we are wronged!" Irina's voice rose. "Our packmates are abducted, tortured, turned against one another, *killed*, and you want to sit back and let other people deal with it?"

"We have lost too much against this enemy already." It was the older woman who spoke. "When I was young, I too might have demanded that justice be served with my own hands. But I am older now, and I see that preserving the pack is more important than standing watch over the whole world myself."

Stoyan shook with fury, "This isn't the whole world. This was our pack who was hurt, and it is taking vengeance against the one who did it. We should be there. We should know that we have avenged our packmates." He shot a look of pure hatred at Karliman. "Especially as we failed to protect or rescue them."

Karliman's eyes narrowed.

"Stoyan," the younger man pleaded. "Please. Please try to understand."

"I do understand," Stoyan spat. "I understand that we prefer to sit back and let everyone else dispense justice and protect us. And you know what that makes us?"

"Smart," Karliman replied, cutting him off. "It makes us smart, and it keeps us alive. Which is why you and Irina will come back to the pack and stay out of this."

Stoyan and Irina both froze. They turned, with shocked faces, to look at one another.

Nathan felt his heart sink. These two had the potential to be powerful. If they came with him, they could be everything they had ever dreamed, and would not have to bow their head to a leader who counseled cowardice.

But it was a powerful thing, to be offered a pack.

"I spoke for you," the boy said. He must be Stoyan's younger brother. He looked at Stoyan with a mixture of adoration and pleading. "I told them that you had done what any of us might do to save Irina."

Stoyan turned his head away. His hands were clenched.

"All of this can be put behind us," Karliman offered silkily. "I am sure that what you saw will show the others why I advised them to stay out of this."

Nathan waited for the acceptance he was sure was coming. But Irina surprised him, "We will consider your offer."

"*What?*" Karliman stared at her.

"Have you not just offered us a place back in the pack?"

Irina reached out to take Stoyan's hand. "We will consider it."

Karliman hesitated. He could not refuse, not without seeming petty. But losing these two, having them choose to leave again, would be another blow to his power.

"Decide quickly, then," was all he said before he stomped away.

Catalonia, Spain

Edgardo Sanchez kept his eyes on the road and his hands wrapped tight around the steering wheel. The roads were dangerous at this time of night, especially in a truck this heavy. The edge of the road could easily vanish into mud—or nothing. Not to mention, this was the time of night when people seemed to get crazy and drive much too fast on these back roads.

In the back, twelve men in full riot gear sat silently on crates of weapons as the truck jolted over the dirt roads. All of them had weapons ready to use at a moment's notice.

Behind the truck were six more just like it. The men in them were on call 24/7, ready to go to any client who needed increased security at a moment's notice. They had guarded celebrities and politicians without asking any questions. They had done hostage rescues. Some were assassins. They were consummate professionals, every one of them.

They had been assured that this job would be unlike anything they had ever seen.

Edgardo had driven these men often, and he doubted that the job would be as different as their client seemed to think it was. He had heard some of the stories while the men were joking with one another after missions, hyped up on adrenaline.

What could they be guarding against here that these men hadn't seen before? They'd seen missiles, terrorists, kidnappers, angry mobs, and more.

Edgardo smiled. These men would earn their paychecks, every cent of them, and it would be another victorious story to tell. Their client had been adamant about secrecy, but he had nothing to worry about.

Behind him, the caravan of armored trucks crawled over the hills of Catalonia, making for the castle they were supposed to guard.

Just let anyone *try* to get into that castle. They wouldn't stand a chance.

Jennifer tossed and turned, trying to get comfortable on the cot. The clock at the edge of the room said it was 2am, which meant she'd been trying to get to sleep for three hours.

She sat up with a groan and rubbed her scalp. It reminded her of Denver here—the dry air quickly losing the day's heat. It should feel familiar.

It didn't.

Everything about this place was strange, down to the locks on the scientists' doors.

Locks that kept them in.

Jennifer had never liked being locked inside, and both times they'd brought her here and locked the door behind

NATALIE GREY & MICHAEL ANDERLE

her, she had to fight the instinctive urge to pull the door off its hinges and beat the security guard to death with it.

Which would kick things off much sooner than they'd planned.

She rolled her head slowly, trying to relax enough to sleep. With the attacks coming tomorrow evening, she needed to be rested.

Maybe if she walked around a bit. She got up and paced around the room a few times. It only made her feel caged, so she leaned on the windowsill and rested her head on the bars, looking out into the hills beyond the valley.

She tilted her head to the side. A caravan was making its way down the roads, moving slowly.

"ADAM? What's that?"

>>What is what?<<

"Sorry. There are…" Jennifer squinted and counted. "Seven trucks in the hills. Is that supplies for the town, or what?"

>>One moment. Analyzing satellite data.<<

She waited, chin propped on her hands. The window was high as well as barred, to make it even more difficult to escape. It wasn't a serious concern in her case, but it would definitely keep someone like Hsu in.

>>They appear to be armored personnel carriers.<<

Jennifer stood up quickly. "Our side, or Hugo's?"

>>As far as I know, they aren't ours. I'll check with Stephen.<<

"Yes. Let him know." Jennifer rubbed at her temples. "Crap. How many people would be in there?"

>>I'll do as much research as I can, and I will let you know as soon as I have answers.<<

"Thanks."

But that meant she now had a bad development...and nothing to do but sit and wait for other people to research it and adjust the plan.

She was never getting to sleep now.

>>**Stephen?**<<

Stephen sat bolt upright in bed, "What is it?"

>>**Jennifer has spotted seven armored personnel trucks coming into the valley.**<<

"Son of a—" Stephen was up and buttoning a shirt within seconds, striding out into the main room. "All right, you lot of geniuses, we need surveillance!"

Bobcat, Marcus, and William appeared, squinting in the suddenly-bright lights of the main room.

"What's going on?"

"Hugo's moving troops in," Stephen told them grimly. "Any numbers, ADAM?"

>>**Based on the size of the trucks, I would say they hold between ten and fourteen occupants each. A relevant question is whether they have been retrofitted to carry bombs or other weaponry.**<<

"Yes, very relevant. Tell me if you figure it out and where they end up going. And let Nathan know that now would be an excellent time to come back with a large group of angry Wechselbalg."

>>**Anything else?**<<

"Nothing yet, although they should be careful getting back into town. I trust you'll be in contact with *ArchAngel* to make sure the Pods don't end up in the middle of the convoy?"

>>**Of course. Unless you think it would be better to head them off now.**<<

Stephen crossed his arms and narrowed his eyes at the map. Ocular implants showed him where the convoy currently was.

"Hard to say," he replied finally. "On the one hand, if we head them off now, before he has a chance to get them into defensible positions, that's good…"

"That does sound good," Marcus agreed.

"On the other hand, having them in the facilities as new staff means it would be almost impossible for Hugo to use the captive Wechselbalg effectively."

"Oh. I hadn't thought of that," Marcus admitted.

"Although it means we have to be absolutely sure that the two facilities can't communicate *and* that there are no automated systems these guards can use to kill the Wechselbalg—like poison."

>>**I'm working on that; all of those should be down by tomorrow at midday.**<<

"Good. Then, as I see it, our basic plan remains unchanged. A few humans with guns won't bother us. If we find out they have bioweapons or something, that would be a different concern, but otherwise, I don't think there's any reason to—"

>>**Stephen?**<<

"What?"

>>**Two of the trucks are heading for the point Bobcat designated for shoe pickup.**<<

"Shit!" Bobcat pounded the table. "They're hoping to get

us while we extract the shoes. We can't let them get away with that."

"If they're shipping containers, shouldn't they be fairly easy to extract?"

Bobcat paused, "Not with the anti-tracking devices we need to install. Plus, I have, ah…"

"What?" William looked at him.

"Nothing. It's just that location is very important to me."

"Well, then come up with a way to get in there that takes those soldiers into account," Stephen advised, "or this whole thing is going to go south really quick." He shook his head. "I just don't get why they're focusing there."

Bulgaria

>>Two are at the area where Bobcat, William, and Marcus will extract the shoes, two more are going to the castle, and three are going to the facility where Jennifer is.<<

"Thank you, ADAM." Nathan made his way through the forest, toward the distant shapes of Irina and Stoyan, heads close together as they spoke.

The time for decision-making was past.

Both of them looked at him as he came out of the trees with Peter at his side.

"Seven trucks full of soldiers just pulled into the town where the facility is," Nathan explained. "I need to leave, to be a part of the strike team."

Irina swallowed, "So you're not taking us?"

"Both of you are more than welcome to join us. But I can't wait any longer."

Stoyan dropped his head into his hands. Leaving the pack had been one of the worst moments of his life. He never wanted to go through that again, to know that the life and family he'd had while growing up were lost to him forever.

If he left, his brother would be crushed. Ivan hadn't come with him to Velingrad—in fact, he had argued strongly against Stoyan going.

Ivan was a rule-follower, someone who prized the harmony of all over anyone's personal desires. He had not accepted Stoyan's argument that the safety of the pack rested on eliminating their enemies.

He would never forgive Stoyan for this.

He looked at Irina. "What will you do?"

"I'm going with him." She nodded to Nathan.

"Is it so easy to decide?" Stoyan shook his head.

"Easy? It feels like my heart is being ripped out. But you heard him." She looked at Nathan and Peter. "They serve someone who doesn't sit back and hide when her people are hurt. Karliman would say that it doesn't even matter what happened to me or anyone else. He would say it's not worth fighting because we might not win. But that's not why I fight. I fight because it's the *right* thing to do."

"You always had the knack of making things clear." Stoyan nodded. "I'm in."

Catalonia, Spain

"That was delicious." Arisha tipped her head back to look at the sky. "What *time* is it?"

"2am." Gerard looked at her with a forced smile.

He was not pleased. The look of fear in her eyes when he first saw her had been delicious, but she was proving more difficult to intimidate than he had hoped.

At the first restaurant, he had questioned her sharply on her whereabouts in Sofia, but the bitch must have seen him somewhere because she knew when he'd come back to the hotel. She swore she had called to him, but he'd ignored her, and so she had gone back to Moscow—and she said everything with a simplicity that was difficult to interpret.

She didn't over-protest her innocence. She didn't use the wide-eyed look women often used when they lied.

So, he tried being nice.

Everywhere they went that evening, people bent over backward to make sure Gerard was happy. Bottles of rare wines and special dishes were brought to their tables, and

NATALIE GREY & MICHAEL ANDERLE

waiters practically sprinted to the kitchens to accommodate any request they made.

And through it all, Arisha took notes, damn her. Like she actually was a travel writer. She asked him about his favorite dishes. She asked him if there were little villages near the coast that were easily accessible.

At first, he played into the ruse because he thought she would break eventually. With every glass of wine, he asked a few more questions...and yet she never slipped up.

"Well, I'm very glad I chose this town." Arisha called his attention back with a happy sigh. "This has been a perfect night, you know. You'll have Russian tourists flocking here by the dozens."

The truth was, she hoped this column would let her keep her job. She hadn't told her boss when she left Sofia, and she had entirely forgotten to send the column. Her inbox was probably full of angry emails by now, and a few hysterical ones from her mother and father.

She was trying not to think about that. If she could just send this lovely article about Spain, listing the wonderful wines and seafood dishes she'd tried, with no requests for reimbursement, maybe her boss would forget that she'd run off. After all, she couldn't really lose this job.

She frowned, realizing she was still thinking as if nothing had changed.

Maybe the truth was that she was worrying about keeping her job because she wanted more than anything to join TQB, and she was afraid they wouldn't let her. She wasn't a fighter. She was just a reporter, and what good was that to anyone?

She was so involved in her thoughts that she didn't

notice Gerard had led her into a dead-end alley...and before she knew it, she was up against a wall with his fingers squeezing at her throat.

"Let's dispense with the pleasantries, shall we?" He was smiling at her. "Tell me everything you know about the bitch."

"Who?" Arisha choked out. She was frozen with fear. He wasn't *really* trying to cut off her air supply, yet.

She should have left after the first restaurant. She should have watched where she was going. She shouldn't have let him give her wine. Regrets piled up in her head, sapping her strength even further.

"You know exactly who I mean." He wasn't smiling anymore.

"I really don't! Please! Who is 'the bitch'?"

"You *aren't* working with TQB?" He punctuated his words with a squeeze of his fingers. "You're not serving the Queen Bitch, herself? You weren't there at Velingrad?"

So, *that* was what TQB stood for?

Too late, Arisha realized he'd seen the flare of recognition in her eyes.

"Do you know what I do to people who lie to me?" Gerard asked her quietly. His hands began to push her down toward the ground. "You had better hope you can convince me to spare your life, Arisha."

She stared up at his face. Something about it seemed...off. Surprising.

Yeah, because right now *is the time to be worried about that.*

And then she realized what it was: he actually felt wronged. He felt personally betrayed that a woman he'd tried to prey upon might have had her own aims—for instance, to free the people he was torturing.

Her regrets disappeared. She was furious.

On the *ArchAngel*, she had watched as the Queen's soldiers sparred and trained. They were all so graceful and beautiful, and Arisha knew that she would never have their skill. But, to her surprise, one of the human recruits had taken her aside and shown her a few moves—ugly brawling moves that would take her opponents down if she moved quickly and decisively.

Treat it, the recruit had said, *as if you only get one shot.*

He'd stopped pushing down so hard when she'd stopped fighting him. She launched herself up, giving him no time to react before her fist caught him right in the sternum, or close, anyway.

She'd missed. *Shit.*

But she knew what to do now. The longer this dragged on, the better his odds of winning grew. She had to take him down quickly. Arisha spun as she raised her elbow to drive it into his temple. It caught him in the shoulder instead, but he still gave a muffled yell of pain as he leaned sideways.

That emboldened her. She grabbed his shirt and dragged his torso upright, then down to meet her knee. She didn't like to think of herself as a violent person, but she knew some of the things Gerard had done for Hugo— and she could just tell the sort of things he liked to do in his spare time. Hurting him felt good.

She decided not to worry about the larger moral implications right now.

He swung at her and missed, staggering sideways, and

she pivoted, lashing out with the other to hit him in the shins. He went down with a yell.

Then a knife appeared in his hand.

"I am going to kill you," he told her, and for the first time since she'd met him, there wasn't any joke in his voice, there wasn't any psychotic smile. He hated her.

He wanted her dead, and he had killed before.

Run, the recruit had told her in training. *The people you might be up against when you're with TQB? You probably won't win if you have to fight. Run, and make all the fuss you can to get somewhere safe and not let your enemies drag you away. Just try to cripple them, and run like hell.*

Her sense of vengeance wanted to get him on the ground and beat on him until he cried, but she knew they had been right. She wasn't one of the Queen's soldiers, and she wasn't like Jennifer or Stoyan or any of the rest—she couldn't tear anyone to shreds.

She ran, stumbling over cobblestones, and in terror, she heard Gerard running after her, grunting with pain as he came down on the leg she'd kicked.

Across one street was a tiny alcove, a place you might miss if you weren't paying attention. Arisha scooped up a rock from the ground as she ran, turned into the alley and wedged herself into the alcove ...and threw the stone down a nearby street. It skittered and bounced as if someone had kicked it.

Gerard didn't hesitate as he followed the noise. He limped past, murder in his eyes, and Arisha sagged with relief. Now she just had to get back to the apartment, but that was in the other direction from the way Gerard had gone.

NATALIE GREY & MICHAEL ANDERLE

And it hadn't been a useless expedition in the least. With a small smile, Arisha unclenched her hand and stared down at Gerard's phone with a satisfied smile.

It was 2:30am when Stoyan, Irina, Nathan, and Peter arrived at the apartment.

Stephen looked up with a nod and a smile. "Glad to see you're both still with us."

Irina nodded back. She didn't trust herself to speak. She knew Karliman's ultimatum had set her free. The pack was never going to change, and the others were not going to come with her. However, knowing that they would not intervene, no matter the stakes, no matter who was being hurt or killed—she could no longer be a part of that.

The truth was it had been just as hard to walk away the second time as it was the first. In some ways, it had been more difficult.

The first time, she knew she was giving up her pack status and they'd cast her out. The second time, though, they'd offered her a chance at what they considered redemption.

But when Stephen had been genuinely pleased to see both her and Stoyan, Irina knew that they had made the right choice. A new pack filled with those who had a shared sense of honor was worth more than her birth pack, who let their kin die without even trying to save them. This was their home now, and it felt more like home than her old pack ever had.

Stoyan was looking around in increasing consternation.

He eased the door open to each of the bedrooms and peered in.

"Where's Arisha?"

"She's sleeping," Bobcat told him, jerking his head toward the door to her room. "Hasn't stirred, even though we've been talking."

"She's not in there," Stoyan growled dangerously.

Everyone stopped dead.

"She's not?" Stephen asked.

Stoyan gritted his teeth, "Look for yourself if you want." He pushed the door open all the way.

"Shit." Stephen grabbed his gun off the table. "Come on. We'll sweep the town and—"

The door to the apartment opened and Arisha slipped in. Her hair was disheveled and there was dirt on her jeans, but she was smiling.

For a moment, no one spoke.

"Um…." Bobcat grunted finally.

"I was out with Gerard," Arisha explained.

Stoyan exploded. "You what?"

"Yeah, he took me around...and then he tried to kill me."

"Yet you're surprisingly upbeat," Stephen observed.

"Well, he didn't kill me. And… I got his phone." She held it up with a smile. The smile faded a moment later. "Of course, I didn't kill *him*, either."

"He tried to kill you?" Stoyan pulled her into a rough embrace. "He tried to…"

Bobcat picked his way around the outside of the hug and tugged the phone out of Arisha's hand. "I'll start running history on this, see which towers it's pinged over the years. Hopefully, we'll get some more facility locations from this bad boy."

"Good idea," Stephen agreed. "And maybe we need a buddy system for tomorrow."

"What are we, four years old?" Peter gave him a look.

"Arisha went missing and yet none of us knew about it," Stephen pointed out. He could have kicked himself, the thought of losing another new member of the team was chilling. "Stoyan, Irina. Don't go off on your own. Arisha…"

He raised his eyebrows. Arisha and Stoyan were *very* thoroughly occupied.

"Ah...huh. I think it's time for everyone to go to bed. We'll cover the whole 'not going off on your own' thing in more detail tomorrow. Goodnight, everyone."

Hugo turned as Gerard quietly entered the room.

He was annoyed. Gerard should have been here. None of them had heard anything from the man for hours. Did Gerard think he could just waltz off and take a long dinner whenever he pleased? While there were truckloads of weapons inbound, and TQB's people might have discovered where they were?

His eyes traveled coldly over the dirt and tears on Gerard's clothing, and the limp the man walked with.

"What happened to you?"

"Nothing." Gerard was not going to admit a failure. Hugo was angry enough, and Arisha's escape still rankled.

How the hell had an untrained woman gotten away from him?

It didn't matter. He reached for his phone and stopped.

His pocket was empty.

Shit.

Hugo noticed his look. "Is something wrong?"

"No," Gerard replied shortly. He nodded to the screens along one wall, and the security guard speaking quietly into a headset. "What's happening?"

If you had been here on time, you would know, Hugo's look said. "We're going to take care of those weapons before they reach this town."

The other trucks caught up with him about an hour before dawn, and Maurice started over the border with a sense of grim determination. They were ahead of schedule now, and the holdup—such as it was—hadn't been his fault. He drove first along the narrow roads and up into the hills. It was pretty country, visible as the sky started to grow lighter. Maybe everything was going to work out, after all. Which was his last thought before he saw the car.

Sleek but heavy, it raced toward him along the road, weaving across the lines. It sat high on large wheels, and the dull siding looked almost like armor plates.

Maurice squinted through the windshield. A drunk driver? A drunk driver in an armored car?

But where he would normally be amused, he was now worried. There were ditches on either side of the road, and the truck was hardly maneuverable, anyway. While he'd likely survive a crash against a car that small, he knew that his instincts might at any moment cause him to swerve and roll the truck into the ditch. The closer the car got, the more it looked like it was *trying* to worry him—like it was coming for *him.* Which meant it was trying to disrupt this shipment.

He didn't know how to outdrive an armored car. Maurice gripped the steering wheel with clammy hands and prayed to every saint he could name to keep him on the road and safe. He could see another car behind this one now.

His radio crackled. "Someone trying to drive me off the fucking road!"

Shit, shit, shit. They were getting closer and he couldn't decide what to do. Try to hit them dead on? Maybe if he played chicken, they would swerve instead of him. But what if they had guns? What if they had grenades? Why the hell had he gotten into this? He stared down the car and moved the truck into the middle of the road. If he tried to avoid them while they tried to kill him, he was going to die. Trying to bring the fight to them, that was his only chance. That was what he told himself, anyway.

About ten seconds out now, by his guess. Nine, eight—

The lead car suddenly spun and rolled, as if it had hit some invisible object. Behind it, the companion car started to fishtail on the dry, open road.

Maurice's mouth hung open.

The first car hadn't even righted itself, but somehow it moved sideways off the road, wheels spinning uselessly in the air and slid into the ditch. The other car, swerving out of control, followed a moment later. It spun in the air—

though why, Maurice couldn't tell, and landed directly on top of the first car.

"Did anyone else see that?" He wasn't sure he'd even managed to say words. What the *hell* had just happened? "Tomas? Are you alright?"

"Yeah." The driver of the back truck sounded just as shell-shocked as Maurice. "It was as if… As if someone just picked the car up and tossed it off the road."

"What the fuck just happened?" Maurice demanded.

"I don't know." Seban, the driver of the middle truck, sounded determined and freaked out in equal measure. "Let's just get the hell out of here and get the trucks where they're supposed to be. I want this job to be over."

"The cars are down," Phillips reported. She looked over her shoulder, expecting to see the General. Her eyes went wide when she saw, instead, the Queen Bitch herself.

"Good work," the Queen told him with a decisive nod.

"I, ah… Your Majesty."

"You don't need to call me that." Bethany Anne smiled briefly at Phillips, then narrowed her eyes at the screens. Her arms were crossed over her chest. "Any read on those cars?"

Phillips swallowed hard. "ADAM's running everything, but we still don't know much." She was still in awe that the Queen herself was here. She'd seen her the other day, of course, talking with Stephen and the others, but she'd never assumed she would meet Bethany Anne. The woman cut an enviable figure in black jeans, black-and-silver heels, and a red shirt that highlighted a perfect figure.

"Let me know as soon as you find out," Bethany Anne requested simply. She looked at Phillips. "I want to know which group of backward goat-fucking micro-cocked village idiots tried to blow up my fucking shoes. Good job, by the way."

And she disappeared into thin air.

Phillips blinked at the air in front of her and then turned back to her desk. She caught herself looking back over her shoulder as she typed, but the Queen did not reappear.

"ADAM? Any read on those armored cars?"

>>I may have a lead. I'll tell Bethany Anne as soon as I know.<<

"Thank you," Phillips replied. She looked over her shoulder again. "Does she do that disappearing thing a lot?"

Lance passed by with a coffee cup. "Fairly often. Try to get used to it, Phillips. And as you may have guessed from this encounter, *don't* use boring swears in her presence."

"Yes, sir."

Catalonia, Spain

At home, Jennifer usually began the day with grumbling, seven or eight cups of coffee, and dire threats against anyone who tried to interact with her for about three hours after waking up.

So far, Stephen was the only one to try to engage her in conversation first thing in the morning and emerge unscathed. He succeeded because he had the sense to bring her a mug and an entire coffee pot when he came to talk to her.

It was the little things.

Her first morning in the facility, Jennifer had tried very hard not to murder anyone. It had been one of the most difficult tasks she had performed in service to Bethany Anne, though she suspected that it was not the sort that would win any medals. She'd grabbed a cup of coffee, plastered a smile on her face, and glided quickly to her laboratory while pretending not to hear anyone's greetings.

This morning, however, when the guards came through

to unlock the doors, Jennifer was almost whistling, she was so happy. This was not only her last day in this godforsaken place, this was *everyone's* last day. By midnight tonight, the rest of the Wechselbalg would be free, being patched up aboard the *ArchAngel*, and Hugo and Gerard would be dead.

"Good morning, ADAM."

>>**Good morning, Jennifer.**<< There was a pause. >>**You've never wished me good morning before.**<<

Jennifer informed him, "I reserve that for special occasions. How goes your progress?" She stood up and shed the baggy blue pajamas each of the scientists were issued—ugly by any standards—and pulled on her shirt and pants.

>>**As you noted last night, Hugo has increased his security. Camera footage shows thirty-six new guards both here and at the prospective pickup point for the shoes, and twenty-four new guards at the castle.**<<

"Look at that, more playmates." Jennifer grinned. "And here I was beginning to think this wasn't going to be a challenge at all."

>>**In addition, Gerard's phone has given us six more potential locations of facilities.**<<

"How'd you get Gerard's phone? Did you hack it?"

>>**Arisha stole it.**<<

"I always knew I liked her. I'll bet he's hopping mad about that. Anything else?"

>>**Not much to report at present. I've begun preparations to sever the connection and establish a radio blackout between the two buildings as soon as the attack begins.**<<

"Well, good luck with that, then." Jennifer whistled as

she laced up her boots. She swung a lab coat on around her shoulders, buttoned it, and stepped out into the hallway. "Now. *Coffee.*"

Thomas Stockton strode around the outside of the castle, his gaze fixed on the walls and sometimes taking in the hills and cliffs surrounding the place. Though it was old, the castle had been built to be defensible. It had the high ground, and the stone walls and heavy double doors into the courtyard were hardly going to be kicked down.

All in all, a good place to fight.

Their commander, Jamie, had come from meeting the big boss and gave a tiny shake of his head to indicate: *this guy is really crazy.*

Apparently, the man who hired them thought they were all going to get attacked by a pack of wolves.

They'd had a good laugh at that one, but quietly, and only in their own space. You didn't laugh at clients, and you definitely didn't tell them that their paranoia was crazy. Especially when that paranoia paid the bills.

"Maybe his family got killed by wolves or something," one of the guys had suggested as they cleaned their weapons last night after arriving. "You know, hiking or whatever. He's just still scared of them."

It seemed as good an explanation as any. Thomas hadn't even known there *were* wolves in Catalonia, but a fear like that didn't come out of nowhere, did it?

Whatever was coming—because there were also whispered reports of trucks with weapons—it had the potential to break up a string of boring jobs, and he hoped it did. He'd signed on here because the Royal Army was too restrictive. You were never able to really go after the bad guys. You just knew they were out there waiting to kill you, but all the bureaucrats had a bunch of rules about what you could and couldn't do.

Private security forces were much better that way. Someone tried to kill your client, you got to go after them however you wanted. The clients had more money than he could properly get his head around, too, so they were never in legal trouble. Thomas heard about a couple of missions that had never hit the news, even with full shootouts and grenades, and that was really saying something.

So far, though, it had been just as boring here as it was in the army. Maybe this would be the job. Maybe.

He completed his circuit of the castle and went back in through the double doors, which were standing open right now.

"Best place to get in would be the back right corner," he told his commander. He pointed. "It's a dark spot in the cameras, so you could probably do it without floodlights coming on."

"Good work," the man told him with a nod. "Anywhere else to worry about?"

"Not really." Thomas shook his head. "Once the doors are closed, there's no getting into this place without climbing the walls, and that'll set off the alarms. I mean, they could land a helicopter in the courtyard, but that isn't going to be quiet; we'd have advance notice."

"Good. I tell ya, anyone would have to be crazy to try to get in here—and since we came in last night, they won't know we're here yet." Jamie gave a satisfied smile. "Should be easy to mop them all up."

Stephen came out of the shower, dripping as he padded over to the bed. It was only a couple of hours past dawn, but the air was beginning to heat already.

He pulled a slim-fitting tank on over his head and over that, a prototype of Jean Dukes' newest body armor. It was thin, and though it might have been heavy for a human, it didn't bother Stephen at all. He tested the motion of it to make sure the straps were properly adjusted and smiled. Jean did good work.

Black pants paired with boots that were easy to move in but not as clunky as standard combat boots and a light-weight black shirt finished off the first proper layer of his battle outfit.

Then he started with the weapons.

He'd had a new harness made for this fight, for a specific reason—he was carrying over twice as many weapons as usual. His guns were side holstered, as per usual, and Jennifer's both lay crossways across the small of his back. Two knives were strapped to each leg, three of them short and perfectly balanced for throwing, one of them a small—but surprisingly effective—combat knife. The grips were slightly too small for his hands.

But perfect in Jennifer's.

Jennifer, an eminently capable warrior even without transforming, had inspired him to precise, standard combat tactics. His knife, large and heavy, an upgraded version of the knife John had carried in the US military, went along the outside of his right calf, hidden under his pant leg. Stephen generally had no need for knives. He preferred to use his claws, but there were occasionally times and places when revealing his powers wasn't the best idea.

Like, for instance, a sleepy Spanish town that didn't yet know it was filled with mythological creatures.

Stephen swung on his coat and went out into the main room for coffee. He caught himself taking down two mugs and smiled slightly. He and Jennifer would be together again tonight.

He had nothing to worry about, he told himself. Her impulsiveness in battle was underlain with good instincts and even better skill. She was not going to be in any real danger, even with the extra guards in place. ADAM had identified which lab was hers and Stephen intended to go there first.

He sipped his coffee.

"Jennifer?"

Her answer came at once, *"Yes?"*

"Good morning."

"It is a good morning, isn't it?"

Stephen stopped with his cup halfway to his mouth. "You're having a good morning and I'm not there to see it?"

"I know, it's a shame. I'll do my best to have a good morning when you're around sometime."

Stephen smirked. "Yeah, I have some ideas for that."

He couldn't hear her laughter, not exactly, but he could feel it.

"*I'll consider that a promise,*" she told him when she'd stopped laughing. "*See you soon.*"

———

The buzz of the machines echoed off the stone walls as Sergio writhed on the floor of a cage.

Hugo watched, trying to hide both his smile and his anticipation. The transformation was coming. Sergio always tried to hold out, but he was never able to resist in the end. The wait almost made it better.

Hugo had never liked to rely entirely on anyone. Not his father, not Gerard, not any of his guards or stewards. He didn't even like relying on his scientists. They had worked for years now without making many break-throughs, and he was getting tired of waiting.

He'd decided to do his own experiments.

Sergio made an excellent candidate. As someone who had never been satisfactorily broken, he was clearly a failure on the scientist's part. He'd been one of the earliest ones, implanted with a chip the way all of the experiments were at Velingrad. The chip, lying against the brainstem, was thought to amplify the effects of the radio waves, although Velingrad had no better results than any other facility.

Something to remember.

Sergio's transformation came at last with a howl, and then a low-voiced rumble of hatred. The wolf crouched for a moment before starting to pace, yellow eyes fixed on Hugo.

Hugo felt a thrill, half-pleasure and half-fear. He had

NATALIE GREY & MICHAEL ANDERLE

won, and both of them knew it—but without the cage, Sergio was still dangerous. That was why he could not yet be used. His transformations and his obedience could eventually be forced, but it would take a long time for them to trust him in battle. He could easily turn on someone before they could set him on his target.

The scientists had cautioned Hugo not to keep the waves running for too long. They were worried about mental deterioration, along with any number of other side effects they twittered on about. None of them seemed to understand that they weren't here to become Nobel prize winners. They were here to make obedient warriors. Most still seemed hung up by the ethical guidelines they had used in the past, and he wondered how much this impeded their research. If he ever found out it had been seriously obstructed, they were going to have a lot to answer for.

His eyes still locked on the beast's, he began to turn the dial up. The command waves beat through the room: *submit.*

Sergio fought it. He paced, he shivered, he yipped.

But at last, he was on his back with his throat bared.

"Good." Hugo smiled. "Now stay there. You can get up when I say."

He left the room, the waves still turned up to their highest setting. He would break Sergio, he vowed. And then he would show the scientists exactly what to do.

Sergio struggled to maintain a single shred of himself. The waves beat against his mind until he thought he would go mad. How the scientists could stimulate anger and pain with simple radio waves, he wasn't sure. He just knew that they could, and that he could only hold out for so long before he snapped. He had never given up hope, he had never stopped fighting, but he wondered now if this would ever end. The pain ate at him slowly but surely.

He breathed shallowly, heart racing.

Submit, submit, submit.

He would not give up. If he died, it would be with his mind intact. Slowly, battling every order, Sergio rolled and struggled to his feet. He panted with pain, but he'd done it. He made armor of his anger. He let it drive him, and even knowing that Hugo was gone from the room, he threw himself at the bars of the cage, snapping his jaws, just to see if he could.

He could.

When he lay down once more, throat bared, it was with a purpose—Hugo didn't know that Sergio still had his mind. He couldn't know. He wouldn't know. Until it was too late.

Gerard was on the parapet watching the new reinforcements when Hugo found him. He forced himself to bow. He had seen Hugo's increasing bad humor, and he knew what happened when a Marcari turned on one of his servants.

He could still see his father's body when he closed his eyes.

Something that felt astonishingly like hatred washed through him and he struggled for control. He would not allow himself to fall into that trap. Sacrifices had to be made if you wanted to stand at the right hand of a king. If you wanted to have power.

And Gerard wanted power.

"How are the new guards?" Hugo asked him. He seemed very pleased, though Gerard did not know why. No good news had come in during the past few days.

"Well trained. I would recommend that we see about replacing our existing guard rotation with these if finances allow."

"Truly?" Hugo raised his eyebrows in surprise. "And what of our existing employees?"

"Clerical work," Gerard replied shortly. "They can file reports, check security and news feeds, and serve as messengers and liaisons. They have not failed us willfully, and do not need to be punished, per se. But they are incapable of serving as your guards with the enemies we face."

It was the correct answer, he knew. Hugo liked to believe that he was a benevolent overlord and that he took good care of the commoners he ruled. He also liked to be served by the very best.

"You can feel free to open negotiations," Hugo stated now. "You've done well."

"Thank you, my lord." An extra show of deference never went amiss. Hugo smiled.

"Before you do that, I would like you to go to the laboratories. Make sure that the guards there are familiar with all of the defensive systems they *should* know about." The emphasis was slight. While the guard captains had protocols of which buttons to push in case of a breakout, even they did not realize that the facilities could be flooded with poison gas, and they did not know that they might seal some of their own in the hallways with the escaped Wechselbalg.

It was best for guards not to know that sort of thing. That manner of knowledge tended to make people weak, even when it represented what was inarguably best for the majority.

"I will do so, my lord."

"Oh, and one more thing." Hugo smiled. "Tell Dr. Yordan to come to the castle at her earliest convenience. I have made a breakthrough, and require her analysis."

He walked away whistling while Gerard stared after him with a frown.

Hugo had made a breakthrough?

Unlikely.

If Dr. Yordan was smart, she would keep a straight face and not contradict Hugo. But, of course, Gerard hoped she wouldn't know to do that.

The sooner she was out of the picture, the better.

Catalonia, Spain

Gerard found the new scientist in her laboratory. She was looking at her papers with an expression of polite interest. Even if it wasn't today, he decided, eventually she was going to slip up, and he was going to catch her. It might take weeks, but he could be patient when necessary.

She looked up when he came into the room, and he was pleased to see wariness in her eyes. It was good that she knew enough to worry about him and wonder what he wanted. Maybe when this was over, and he had proved she was a traitor, Hugo would let Gerard kill her.

A pleasant thing to think about. He smiled.

"Dr. Yordan, Mr. Marcari would like to see you at the castle."

"Why?"

Gerard stared at her coldly. "It is not your place to question Mr. Marcari. Go now."

He did not wait for her to respond. He left and went to the basement, where the new guards had entirely taken over the barracks. A few of the old guards hurried past him with resentful looks. If they'd been capable, no new guards would have been necessary.

Gerard almost hoped one or two of them would complain so he could make an example of them to the others. Just let them try to whine about this when they were sitting around all day drinking wine and eating pastries. They wouldn't last beyond a minute if the Wechselbalg got loose.

He was pleased to see all of the new guards' nod to him as he came into the room, and they quieted at once. "I've come to see if there's anything I can help with," Gerard began pleasantly. "I see you have the building blueprints there." A carefully edited set of blueprints was provided to the guard captains, conveniently leaving out the defense mechanisms.

"We'd like to patrol each of the floors and make sure the scientists are aware of how we operate," the commander replied. He was a tall man with blond hair thinning ever so slightly on top. "We've found that civilians are more predictable in a crisis if they know exactly where to go and what to expect from us."

Gerard's smile didn't even flicker. "I can certainly arrange for you to meet all of them, perhaps later today in the cafeteria. But, there is a great deal of sensitive research being conducted, and we simply can't allow you access to those floors except in case of emergency."

"With all due respect, sir, we can't efficiently guard places we're not familiar with."

"I can understand that. However…." Gerard gestured to the blueprints, "Not only do you have those, the layout of the middle floors is identical to that of the first floor. If something goes wrong, there won't be any surprises."

"There's more to it than that," the man argued. "Loose floor tiles, flickering lights, exposed pipes—anything and everything can be useful in a fight. We really should see those areas."

"And I can't allow it." Gerard's tone was crisp and cool. "Consider it a condition of your continued employment that you refrain from going to those floors." His gaze swept around the room. "Are we clear?"

To the man's credit, he didn't even hesitate. "Absolutely, sir. I don't mean to cause any trouble."

"Then see that you don't," Gerard directed simply. He left without another word.

If these men continued their employment here—or at least those who Gerard deemed had enough leverage to be kept in line with threats and blackmail—they would see everything. For now, they were temporary and they needed to know their place.

Jennifer made a show of feigning indifference to the soldiers around her as she was led into the courtyard. She kept her hands in her pockets and her eyes straight ahead. But she took in everything through her peripheral vision. Two trucks were together at the edges of the courtyard. The vehicles' interior benches were hollow, and the raised bed of the truck also seemed to hold supplies; she caught the shape of ammo boxes when she turned her head slightly. The men themselves moved well in their armor.

Their gear was expensive, and they handled their weapons with ease. They also had discipline, evident in the fact that not one of them whistled or catcalled. These men wouldn't be easily distracted or frightened.

It *was* going to be somewhat of a challenge. Jennifer allowed herself a small smile. She ascended the stairs at the end of the courtyard and nodded to the butler inside the main doors. It was ridiculous that Hugo had a butler. She was led along corridors, and past a room that emitted a tooth-aching buzz. Jennifer frowned at that, but the butler didn't seem like the type to answer questions.

In Hugo's study, she found him sitting behind his massive desk, smiling broadly. The room was ridiculously opulent, from the mahogany furniture to the priceless rugs and paintings lining the walls. The effect was, Jennifer thought, a little bit like a kid playing dress up.

"You wanted to see me, sir?"

"Yes. Dr. Yordan, I have something exciting to show you. I believe I have made a breakthrough in forcing the beasts to accept me as their Alpha."

"I beg your pardon?" Jennifer knew her voice sounded icy at the use of the word 'beasts,' and she scrambled to recover. "I am sorry, my Catalan is still not so good. I beg your pardon, sir. Did you say you've made a breakthrough? That is very good news." The last words had to be forced out.

I swear, I will kill you with my bare hands. Though the thought of sinking her teeth into him was also a good one...

"Yes." If Hugo was upset by her momentary lapse, he didn't show it. "Come, come. I'll show you."

He led the way back to the strange room, and Jennifer hung back outside the door, suddenly worried. She knew the results of the experiments they had done in these facilities, but she'd never seen one performed.

She found that she really didn't want to.

This will be over tonight, this will be over tonight, this will be over tonight... She walked through the door with a cursory smile.

And her world turned inside out. Pure rage pounded at her, pain assailed her on all sides, and through the haze of everything, she could hear only one command: *submit, submit, submit.*

What the hell was going on here? She raised her head blearily and saw a cage, a wolf prone on its back, throat exposed. It had been forced to obedience, by the very waves that were assaulting her now.

Sudden panic made her want to run from the room. She was going to transform. She was going to transform and she couldn't stop herself.

>>Jennifer? Are you all right? Your heart rate has increased sharply and—<<

But ADAM's words disappeared into a roaring in her ears.

"Dr. Yordan?" Hugo was bending over her.

She must have fallen.

"Dr. Yordan, are you alright?"

"I'm...just..." *Oh, please no.*

But as ridiculous as it was to think of Hugo as her Alpha, as easy as it would be to resist the urge to submit, the urge to transform was still strong. She could feel the change coming, ripping through her, and she could not stop it. She rolled her head, breathing labored, and the last thing she saw before her transformation was the gaze of the other werewolf.

Unwatched by Hugo, clearly understanding what was happening to her, the Wechselbalg had flipped to its feet and stared at her. There was awareness in its gaze—awareness, and self-control.

Jennifer clung to that fact as the room seemed to go pitch black.

>>**Stephen!**<<

"What? What is it?" Stephen jerked up from his last, obsessive scan of the blueprints.

>>**You have to go now. Go to the castle.**<< ADAM's voice was urgent. >>**She's transforming. They ran an experiment on her.**<<

"*What?*"

>>**I don't understand, she didn't ask for my help. I don't know what's happening, there aren't cameras in that room. She's on the second floor after the staircase up from the courtyard. I'm cutting the power now, and the link between the facilities, but you have to go *now*.**<<

"I'm on my way." Stephen ran for the door, yelling for the others.

The room went dark and Hugo stumbled for the light switch near the doorway. He fumbled in the darkness, fingers sliding over stone and plaster. Dr. Yordan was sick; he had to get the lights on and get her help. One of his foremost researchers could not be lost. He was still fumbling when he heard the rattle of the cage door and his blood turned to ice.

Oh, no. He turned with his heart in his throat. The power had kept the cage doors closed.

And was he seeing… No, it couldn't be. But he could swear he was seeing *two* pairs of wolf's eyes gleaming in the faint light that came from under the door.

_____

Catalonia, Spain

"ADAM, tell me you have a plan for getting us into that castle!" Stephen pounded down the stairs to the ground floor—and the car Bobcat had pulled around. Rumbling and mean, it was a 1965 Pontiac GTO that Lance and Bobcat had practically drooled over.

Stephen couldn't have cared less right now. Hell, he'd be happy with a rabid camel if it got him to the castle in good time.

>>**Pucks.**<< ADAM replied succinctly.

"What?"

>>**Pucks. With nets. It will help you get onto the parapets from the back of the castle—and it will help the car get to the back of the castle.**<<

Stephen relayed this to Bobcat, who muttered, "It had better not scratch the paint job."

>>**You have reinforcements coming as well.**<< ADAM informed Stephen.

"What? Who?"

>>**Tabitha.**<<

"You're kidding me. Right? Tell me you're kidding me."

>>**No. She will join you at the castle.**<<

"This is going to get interesting." Stephen raised his eyebrows.

"Why?" Bobcat called back, over the whistle of the wind.

"Because Tabitha," Stephen, momentarily broke off his explanation, "take a left here, we're going around to the base of the cliffs—Tabitha is going to be joining me at the castle."

Bobcat swore and shook his head. "I always wanted to see her fight in person! I wish I didn't have to go to the drop point."

"Sergio?" Hugo's voice broke on the word.

Jennifer bared her teeth in a smile. The waves that had caused her transformation were gone—now she was just herself, strong, claws sharp against the floor, and teeth ready to sink into flesh. She was a weapon—and she was no one's but her own.

She could almost hear the other wolf's thoughts. More to the point, she didn't need to. The mewling, pathetic human in this room had enslaved their kind, tortured many and killed more than that. He had tried to become their Alpha without ever earning that title.

He had to die. And that death should be painful.

"Dr. Yordan?" Hugo managed.

Jennifer growled.

"Spare...spare the doctor." Hugo tried to give the command, but his terror was laughable.

How had this man ever thought he would be an Alpha? He wasn't even smart enough to realize that she had transformed as well. Jennifer chuffed with laughter, and after a pause, she heard the other wolf make the same sound. His was creaky, as if he had forgotten how to laugh, but he joined in with enthusiasm.

"I want you to know, I did this for a greater purpose!"

Jennifer's wolf eyes, far better in light and dark than human eyes, made out Hugo's shape by the door. He was trying to open it, but was having no luck. The human part of her was thinking about power loss and automatic door locks and whether the castle had been retroactively wired for defense. The wolf part of her didn't care. Her prey was stuck in here with her. That was the important part. A thought occurred and was gone. She wasn't supposed to kill him yet. She just didn't remember why right now. It was hard to remember when she had teeth she could sink into flesh and tear, rip.

"Let me explain!" He was almost crying with terror. "Look at the world, look at the chaos. Look at the wars. People moving everywhere as they see fit, countries clashing. It doesn't need to be that way!"

Jennifer, pacing back and forth, tilted her head to the side. How this related to the torture of Wechselbalg, she could not imagine. What did this man think he could say to avoid his fate?

Sergio apparently did not care. His growl was easily understood by both wolves and humans—pure threat. His claws clicked on the floor as he moved ever closer.

"I will restore the glory of the world." There was a weak rattling sound as Hugo pulled at a doorknob that wouldn't open and gave a hiccupping sob of terror. "Oh, God. Oh, my God. Mercy. *Mercy!*"

His fear was intoxicating, spurring them both onward, and both wolves crouched—

The other facilities. Jennifer's human brain crashed through the wave of instinct. She gave a yip, telling Sergio not to jump, and his head whipped around in disbelief.

Wait.

"*Jennifer? Can you hear me?*" Stephen's voice.

Jennifer gave a questioning growl.

"*Tabitha will be there soon to get the locations from the computers, and Gerard's phone gave us all but one.*" Stephen's voice was tight with fear. "*You can kill Hugo if you see him.*"

She snapped her jaws in pleasure.

His voice changed, softer. "*Are you all right?*"

She yipped.

"*I'll take that as a yes. I'll be there soon.*"

Jennifer turned to the other wolf and yipped again. Every fiber of her being wanted to tear Hugo apart, but it was clear even from a moment she saw Sergio in that cage that he had endured more than she had. Sergio deserved to take his revenge. She took a step backward to make it clear.

"I know you're intelligent." Hugo's voice filtered out of the semi-darkness. "Please—please. You must understand what you are."

Dangerous ground. If Jennifer were in human form, she would have raised an eyebrow. *Tread carefully.*

Although, of course, she hoped he didn't.

"You are blessed by God!" Hugo shouted. "You have

been given incredible talents. When you know your place, when you learn obedience to my will, you will be serving God's higher purpose!"

Sergio gave a growl that was almost a whine, and Jennifer chuffed. She instantly understood what Sergio meant: *I am so done with listening to this shit. Can I kill him now?*

She yipped, and Sergio leapt.

Hugo's scream might have been short. It would have been easy to tear his throat out, after all. But Sergio didn't want it to be quick. His teeth sank into Hugo's shoulder and tore away tissue as his claws raked down the man's arm. With a snap of his jaws, he crushed the bones in Hugo's right hand.

The man screamed in agony.

Sergio took a step backward and nodded his head to Jennifer.

She didn't hesitate. Her attack left him bleeding from scratches across his torso and down onto his thighs. She circled away as he fell to the ground, crying out in pain.

You did this to us. You made us do this to others. How dare you?

He didn't deserve to live. And he didn't deserve to die with dignity, either.

>>**Jennifer, the guards are mobilizing toward your location. I have managed to seal some of them in the courtyard, but there are eight in the building.**<<

God-fucking-dammit.

They could both hear it now. The pounding of boots on the stairs, and the call of commands, along with the low flex and clank of body armor and weapons, a heavy sound.

Sergio, to his credit, was not obsessed with revenge over sense. His leap and the snap of his jaws ended Hugo's screams forever. He and Jennifer tore the body limb from limb, and Jennifer bared her teeth at it. If she were human, she would have spit on him.

>>**Should I unlock the door?**<<

Jennifer yipped.

>>**I need to learn how to understand wolves. Yip once for yes, and twice for no.**<<

She yipped once.

>>**Thank you. Door opening. The guards are climbing the staircase and should be turning into the corridor from your left in fifteen seconds.**<<

Thank you, ADAM. She couldn't say it now, but she'd say it later.

For now, the hunt was on.

"Goddammit!" Jamie yanked at the door to the outside.

This was the sort of thing he'd been worried about, that the various facilities had defensive systems his men couldn't override. Things like doors that automatically locked when the power went out.

If his men failed to protect their employer because of something like this, he was *not* going to take the blame. Rich people always thought they knew best. Especially people descended from the old nobility. Didn't they understand? That world didn't exist anymore! But resentment would get him nowhere, and he was obligated to do his very best to lock the place down. This was just a power failure, but it would serve as a good example of what he needed in a crisis. Mr. Marcari would understand why Jamie and his guys needed to know the buildings they were protecting.

"Upstairs," he ordered curtly. "We need to locate Mr. Marcari and form a defensive perimeter."

The men knew why he was upset and they knew what purpose this response served. They didn't complain, and they didn't half-ass it. Their weapons were readied and they crept forward, covering one another as the group moved through the halls in a leapfrog pattern. Professionals practiced every training mission like it was live. That's why they were the best. They never just went through the motions.

And then the screams started.

The men exchanged a quick look and increased their pace. Fingers twitched near triggers.

"Lab actual, come in," Jamie muttered into his radio. "Lab actual, come in. We have an incident at the castle. Commence lockdown."

Nothing. No answer.

"Courtyard, come in."

Nothing. The men broke into a run.

The wolf seemed to come out of nowhere. It hit Jensen at head height and bowled him backward. The man never had a chance before his life ended in a gurgle, and the wolf crouched as it looked up at them.

Jamie could swear that it *smiled*.

His mouth was dry with fear, but he reacted on an instinct drilled into his muscles for the past fifteen years of his life. He raised his weapon and fired. The bullet caught the wolf in the shoulder, but it didn't even seem to hurt the beast. It was huge, he realized. It should only come to his thighs at *most*, but its shoulder height was well above his hip.

"Fire, everyone fire!" He had to keep control of his men, some of who were staring at Smith's corpse in horror.

The wolves were real. The wolves were *real.*

Or this was a terrible nightmare.

And then there was a growl from behind him.

Shaking, Jamie turned to see another wolf. It was slightly smaller than the first, but its teeth were also dripping with blood. Jamie knew the truth in an instant—their employer was already dead. And they were about to die. He raised his weapon, firing wildly as the second wolf launched itself into him. There was a sharp pain at the joints of his body armor and a burst of pain along his neck, then the world went dark to the sound of screams.

ADAM watched the movement of the bodies through the facility. He was proud of the work he had done. Yesterday he had programmed in a failsafe that would auto-lock any door connected to the main system as soon as there was a power loss. Even when the power came back on, ADAM would be the only one who could open the doors.

Now he watched as figures scurried around the courtyard, trying unsuccessfully to batter their way into the castle. They didn't know what was inside, though. He'd made sure of that.

A combination of Pucks and manipulation of the electrical systems effectively blocked radio communications into and out of both the castle and the laboratory.

They couldn't get out, and they couldn't warn one another.

It was a perfect plan, ADAM thought with satisfaction —and unlike many plans that he thought were perfect until he saw the chaos of human responses to stimuli, this plan was actually going well. He had finally managed to use humans' instincts against them.

>>**Bethany Anne, a status update on the mission. It began early due to an unexpected transformation on Jennifer's part. I've managed to lock the new soldiers inside their respective facilities and lock communications to and from the outside. Operations will take place in the dark to enhance fear in our opponents.**<<

There was a long pause, and then:

ADAM?

>>**Yes?**<<

Just don't turn into Skynet.

Stephen looked up at the wall stretching above him and considered his options. Behind him, the car was being lifted back over the cliff as Bobcat yelled instructions at ADAM, the car, the wind, and the cliff. Stephen's mouth twitched as he tried to hold back a smile. Two Pucks hovered nearby, supporting a tiny ladder.

No sense in waiting around, he supposed. He grabbed the top and settled his feet, and let ADAM lift him to the top of the wall. He hopped down into a crouch on the parapet. Shouts from below indicated that the guards in the courtyard were half-annoyed by their inability to get into the castle and half-worried about causing property damage.

No one seemed sure if this was some sort of drill or an actual encounter. Stephen smiled. None of them were going to know anything until it was far too late.

He turned and made his way quickly toward the stairs that led into the palace itself, a yawning doorway into the black. Castles could be exceptionally dark when they lost power, and Stephen smiled. Any humans locked in the darkness would be subject to a primal sense of fear.

In this case, their fear was entirely warranted. A guard burst out of the darkness. He was splattered with blood, running for his life, and as soon as he was in the sunlight, he started to scream.

"Wolves! *Wolves!*"

His voice carried, annoyingly, on the breeze. There was a sudden silence from the courtyard, and then the attacks on the door redoubled. The guard barely had a chance to notice Stephen, and he was dead a moment later, sliding off Stephen's claws to the ground with blood pooling from his neck.

"ADAM, tell Jennifer to expect more company. The alarm has been sounded. And tell her I'll be there soon." Stephen sprinted into the darkness toward the scent of fear.

14

Catalonia, Spain

As he plunged into the darkness of the castle—dark, at least to human eyes—Stephen could hear the distant snarling of wolves and the terrified screams of the guards.

Once, he might have felt sad for these men. It was their first encounter with the Queen's justice, and they had lived for a long time in a world that did not punish them in the same way.

But those who had been here for years had made the choice to stand by as their employer tortured hundreds, maybe thousands, and those who had just arrived had either made the choice to do the same or made the choice to protect Hugo without learning why someone would want to kill him.

Willful ignorance was no better than willful blindness, and neither would be forgiven.

"ADAM, how many enemies?"

>>In total, there are thirty-seven left in the building. One of the new guards is trying to short out the elec-

trical system on the doors. There are fifteen servants, and sixteen of the other guards—they're not as well trained, but they do have guns. Seven have barricaded themselves in the server room in the subbasement.<<

"Excellent. Thank you, ADAM."

Stephen's eyes registered movement down the hallway and he dropped to a crouch as his assailant fired a wild shot. He muttered, "Let me guess, one of the old guards."

The man deserved to die for stupidity alone. In the darkness, his human eyes could not possibly see if he was firing at an ally or an enemy. He was terrified, trying to use a weapon against an enemy he could neither see nor understand.

He turned to run as Stephen stood, but he didn't get very far before Stephen was on him. He slapped the man and grabbed his gun. The last thing the man saw was the barrel of his own weapon. Stephen fired, dropped the pistol, and kept walking.

Those who didn't understand their own weapons would die by them. That was one of his personal rules.

Deep down, he found himself somewhat disappointed.

Wasn't *anyone* here going to pose a challenge?

It wasn't very nice to toy with your prey, but Jennifer was far past the point of caring whether or not she was nice. She and Sergio pursued the seventh of the guards down the hallway, stalking him, making a show of peeking into the wrong rooms as he sobbed quietly with fear and tried to evade them.

He didn't have the first idea how easily they could kill him if they wanted to. Hopefully, he would lead them to the original guards who had attacked them.

Without silver bullets, these guards weren't a real problem more a massive inconvenience. They could heal through semi-automatic weapons fire, they just didn't particularly want to. It stung like hell, and then it itched, and all in all, it was best not to let that guard sneak up on them.

The question, of course, was where had he gone?

There was a stampede of footsteps drawing closer and Jennifer and Sergio looked at one another with interest. Voices called out commands in Catalan and faltering English, and the soldier screamed something about wolves. The sudden rush of fear in the newcomers rolled down the hall. The new guards with their fancy gear clearly hadn't known about the Wechselbalg, but these other guards knew.

They'd walked past the cages numerous times, and from her lab, Jennifer saw the flash of both satisfaction and fear in their eyes. Humans liked seeing animals caged when they knew those same animals could rip them limb from limb.

As she and Sergio loped toward their prey, they heard the order to stay, and the other shouts to run. Discipline was breaking down, no matter how the guard captain screamed for them to hold ranks.

It doesn't matter, Jennifer wanted to assure him, *you're all going to die anyway.*

Their first kills were the guards who had obeyed orders, pointing guns down the corridor with shaking hands. They fired wildly as Jennifer and Sergio approached.

Jennifer had no desire to find out if these guards carried silver bullets. She wove and leapt, staying under and over the line of fire, and as the burst of firing ended— the terrified men fumbling for magazines—she launched herself into the air to take them out.

They surrounded her, but they did not have the first idea how to use that to their advantage. Circled up, they realized too late that not only could they not shoot—for fear of hitting one another—none of them could grapple with a wolf. Humans liked to hunt in packs, too, but these had never learned how. Jennifer chuffed and took the opportunity to rip an arm off the human directly in front of her. The hysterical screams were almost funny. Hadn't they always known this was going to happen? Hadn't they realized that a human shifter could only be caged for so long before it outsmarted you and escaped?

Apparently not. Jennifer left the first man to bleed to death as she raked the second with her claws. He was trying to run. He really should know that wouldn't help him. The back of his head caved in with a snap of her jaws. The next target was the man who'd successfully managed to reload his pistol.

She dodged sideways as he brought the gun up and took him down with her jaws on the back of his neck, shaking until he went limp. The other two tried to run, and just as Jennifer's muscles bunched to leap after them, a figure in all black kicked one of them.

Claws and red eyes flashed, Stephen drew his hands across in an X as he knelt over his target, nearly severing the man's neck. He shot a grin at Jennifer as he raised a gun, aimed without thought and took down the last of her targets.

She transformed as she ran to him. One moment there was a wolf bounding along the corridor then, with hardly a stumble, there was a naked woman on two feet, flinging herself into his arms.

Stephen went over backward. He didn't care. His fingers tangled in Jennifer's hair and their lips met urgently.

"Hi," Jennifer managed.

"Hello." Stephen grinned at her. "Are you going to be having the rest of this fight naked? Because I think Ecaterina would approve. Also, I brought your guns if you want them."

Jennifer laughed as she hauled him to his feet, "No, it's *way* too fun seeing their expressions when you appear out of the dark as a wolf. But it's kind of hard to hug as a wolf."

"Also, I much prefer kissing you when you look like this," Stephen added. He raised an eyebrow at the man who had transformed behind her. "Hello. I don't believe we've met."

"Sergio," the man replied by way of introduction. He nodded to Stephen. "I don't speak much English. I see you. At Velingrad."

"I can speak Bulgarian." Stephen switched. "You saw me?"

"I was Hugo's...favorite. He had me in the helicopter. I

saw you on the roof." The man looked back and forth between them. "So *you*, Dr. Yordan—you were why he was chasing the helicopter?"

Jennifer looked a little bit ashamed. "Yeah. I...yeah. Also, my name isn't Irina, it's Jennifer."

"I smelled another Wechselbalg on that helicopter, but I thought it was just blood on you." Sergio smiled. "You surprised me."

"Yeah, I also surprised myself. What the hell was going on in that room?"

"He has developed a way to force transformation," Sergio explained. "Surely you knew that much, if you were posing as a scientist."

"I had some help." Jennifer lifted one shoulder. "Also, I didn't know how they did that. I haven't been implanted with anything. Doesn't it require a chip?"

"No, actually. Some labs used chips to enhance the signal, but any Wechselbalg exposed to the signal will be vulnerable."

"I was in the lab for a day and a half, though."

"The labs are shielded so that the experiments don't interfere with one another. If you didn't run any experiments, you wouldn't have been exposed."

"Oh. So how does it work?" She asked.

"They force the shift with that machine and then give commands. It is almost impossible to resist them for long, but he still does not know how to force someone to obey him immediately, except by breaking their spirit. It was why he hated me—even after two years, I did not reliably obey him."

A female's voice called. "GERONIMOOOOOOOO!"

The yell echoed down the hallway and everyone turned to look. There was the sound of things crashing to the floor accompanied by some inventive swearing.

"Oh, didn't I mention?" Stephen spoke to Jennifer. "Tabitha's here."

Gerard frowned. Hugo hadn't answered his cell phone, and he wasn't answering the main line that ran to the castle, either. At the very least, the butler should have picked up. He tried not to worry—after all, the odds were tiny that something could strike the castle so quickly that not a single guard could get the alarm out, and none of the new guards had received so much as a peep on their radios.

But this was unusual, and he didn't like it.

He strode into the guard captain's study, letting the door slam against the back wall. "Show me the security feeds from the castle." The guard captain jumped, but his trembling fingers dutifully pulled up the security feeds.

Gerard frowned at them. Everything seemed entirely normal.

People were moving about in the courtyard without any particular urgency, the butler stood at attention inside the main doors, and servants were moving through the halls to clean. But no one was answering the phone. He lifted the receiver on the guard captain's desk and dialed again. There was a phone next to the butler. The man should have picked up, but he didn't even move. He didn't jump, he didn't so much as glance at the phone.

Gerard counted the rings. By five, Hugo should pick up

the phone, and if he did not, someone else should answer. That was standard. But the butler didn't look over, and he didn't pick up.

"That's weird." The guard captain's voice sounded strained.

"What's weird?" Gerard's head whipped around. He didn't like the sound of that.

"Well, it's just… We can monitor the feed from the power station. And it's still feeding power to the castle. Sort of." The guard captain pointed to his screen. "But the castle is cut off from it."

Gerard looked at the screen the guard captain was pointing at. He looked back at the video feeds. They weren't frozen. People were moving. But if the power was truly off, they should be showing static. He looked back at power station feed. He had a very bad feeling about this.

"You're telling me," he clarified carefully, "that although the castle looks to be running entirely normally here, it's—"

The room went pitch black.

"Lost power," the guard captain finished Gerard's comment.

"Yes."

Tabitha dusted herself off as she walked.

"Fucking vase ripped into my pants when it shattered," she complained.

There was a resounding silence from Ryu and Hirotoshi. Tabitha looked over her shoulder. Both of them had the too-straight faces of men trying not to laugh.

Well, if they were trying to stay quiet, she clearly had no choice but to tease them a bit. "*Totally* the vase's fault."

The corner of Hirotoshi's mouth twitched. It was slight, but she knew she was getting to him.

"I am a paragon of grace and elegance," Tabitha announced.

Ryu gave a pained squeak as he pressed his lips together.

"Busted." She gave him a look as they came around the corner.

"I believe that vase was very valuable," Hirotoshi tried. "Perhaps we should not engage in wanton destruction of property."

Tabitha shrugged. "Well, it's not valuable anymore. Anyway, you know the rule, be a mass-murdering fuckhead and the rest of us don't have to care about breaking your shit."

"However creatively phrased, that is a sound principle," Hirotoshi admitted.

They came around the corner to see Stephen and two naked people.

"Jennifer!" Tabitha waved then looked Jennifer up and down. "Looking *good*."

Stephen stepped in front of Jennifer with a glare at Tabitha. "Can I help you?"

"Oooh, how gentlemanly." Tabitha stuck her tongue out at him. "Or priggish."

He raised an eyebrow, "Priggish?"

She took a step backward.

Ryu leaned forward to whisper in her ear, "You're on your own with this one."

"Oh, that's nice. I thought you were supposed to help me during fights."

"Yes, but I don't have a death wish." He looked at Stephen. "And insulting Stephen's manners is something you only do if you have a death wish. That's common knowledge."

Stephen cleared his throat.

"All right, all right." Tabitha looked pointedly at the wall. "I'm not looking at your naked girlfriend. Will you tell me where the subbasement is?"

There was a pause.

"Down," Stephen answered.

Tabitha rolled her eyes. "You know what I meant. Which way are the stairs?"

"Back of the building." He pointed wearily. "One staircase goes all the way down. And just out of curiosity, why isn't Barnabas here?"

"I'm useful too, you know!"

"Yes, but we need to get information out of these people that may not be in the computers, and Barnabas can read minds."

"So can I!" Tabitha planted her hands on her hips.

Stephen exchanged a look with Ryu and Hirotoshi, both of whom also looked baffled. "You...can?"

"Well, no. But I can shoot people in the kneecaps until they tell me things." Tabitha held up her pistol with a chipper grin. "And that's almost as good. Come on, guys, let's go get some information."

Stephen watched as Tabitha walked off cheerily toward

the stairs. "Just when I think I have the hang of talking with that woman."

"It's good for you," Jennifer informed him. "Sometimes you *are* a prig."

Stephen looked around, "Does no one appreciate me today?"

"It's very endearing," she assured him. "All right, where to?"

"Hugo, I assumed. Unless you've already killed him."

"We did."

"I hope it was painful," Stephen offered quietly. He didn't like this streak of vengefulness—he preferred to act calmly and rationally, and the force of this hatred threatened to tip him into pure rage. On the other hand, if anyone had ever had it coming...

"It was. But not nearly as painful as having to listen to that stupid speech about us learning our places." Jennifer gave Sergio a look. "Did he do that a lot?"

"You have no idea," the other man replied, shaking his head. "That wasn't even the bad part. It was watching sane people go along with it. I even asked some of them why they did, when what he was doing was clearly sociopathic. They just wanted the salary—and they were afraid of getting on Gerard's bad side." He raised an eyebrow. "There's someone else I wouldn't mind a shot at."

"Well, if we do the cleanup quickly, we might get to the other facility before Nathan kills him," Stephen pointed out. "What do you say, sweep the castle and then the courtyard?"

Jennifer nodded, "And they have their armored trucks out there, so we have a good way to get to the facility, even if they're on alert." She paused. "Wait. How'd you get here?"

"Bobcat brought me." Stephen shook his head. "Although it's hardly an armored car. And I think he's working on the shoe pickup."

It wasn't even noon yet, and the clearing was baking hot. Eli Gotten plodded around the area with increasing annoyance.

Who, exactly, had decided that they needed to defend a patch of dirt?

His radio crackled. "Car."

That was more like it. Eli scrambled up the hill to the lookout point and crawled up next to Sean. They squinted at the cloud of dust rising from the car.

"That's not a military car."

Sean gave him a look. "Yeah, but what's it doing out here? This road goes nowhere."

"Maybe a tourist got lost." Eli shrugged. "Either way, it's not—"

Eli's observation came to an abrupt halt as they saw the guided missile streaking toward them.

15

Catalonia, Spain

"Let's hope this wooooooorks!" Bobcat pressed the button on the guided missile system.

The whole car jerked with the force of it, but this was no ordinary launch system. Between the lightness of the missiles themselves and the acceleration the missiles could pick up in the air—an adaptation of the Puck technology— the car didn't flip or bounce seriously the way it would ordinarily have done.

"Good job!" Marcus called over the sound of the wind.

"Aren't you worried they'll shoot at us?" William yelled.

In the backseat, Peter panted slightly as the wind caught his jaws. He hadn't transformed until they were out of town, shedding his clothes while Marcus shielded his eyes in palpable discomfort.

These guys didn't usually fight with them, so they didn't understand the rather unique constraints posed by transformations. But they were looking forward to the fight, he could tell.

Bobcat had been the chauffeur for any number of Bethany Anne's missions, and the guys got to test out the different weapons made by the other engineers on the Meredith Reynolds. But they wanted to get in on the action themselves, and thankfully had agreed to wear body armor and not try any heroics.

Peter was here partially to make sure they kept that promise.

He had enjoyed seeing the soldiers scurry up to the overlook then away again as soon as the missile launched. He was going to enjoy what was coming, too.

An open battlefield added some challenges, and these were apparently elite bodyguards. They knew the deal when they signed up for this job. They knew there was the chance that someone better was going to come along.

Hell, sixteen to one? Peter was giving them a real chance. Somehow, he didn't think they were going to take advantage.

The clearing was surrounded with hills and trees, making it pretty much invisible from the nearby town, even if someone had been watching with high-powered binoculars. It also made the approach into the clearing a blind one, but Bobcat wasn't worried. He turned the wheel sharply and enjoyed the fishtail feel as the car skidded sideways before finding purchase on the dusty gravel.

Driving like this, out on country roads, pushing a car to the limits of its engineering—that was the thing he missed most. He could still do it if he wanted to, of course, but he didn't like to ask Bethany Anne to take him back to Earth for something so small.

He was just going to enjoy the hell out of this now.

The car screamed into the clearing with Marcus and William crouched low in their seats. The convertible didn't really offer much in the way of cover, and Peter suspected that if Stephen hadn't been so focused on getting to Jennifer, he would have argued strongly for the guys to approach the clearing another way.

Peter didn't wait for the car to stop. His muscles bunched, and he jumped, landing partially on one dumb-struck soldier and pushed off again to take down the one trying to run for the trees. He broke the man's neck easily with a swipe of his paw and turned around. This soldier—operating on instinct—had managed to pick up his gun and point it, but he held it backward and was shaking hard enough that he wouldn't have been able to fire it in any case.

Peter batted the gun away and tore his head off with a growl.

Gunfire spattered into the dirt nearby and he took off, weaving through the trees. The brief respite from the sun was welcome—and reminded him of the west, in a way, where he'd learned not to sit in the sunlight in the summer. His fur was made for cold. He noticed, as he came around the edge of the clear, that there was only one truck.

So, eight on one. Well, six now.

A few of them screamed to one another as Peter loped up the hill. Bullets whizzed overhead, but they weren't fast enough to hit home. He sprinted across the uneven terrain, moving faster than the enemies these guys were accus-tomed to.

A knot of four waited for him at the top of a hill. One

went over backward as he approached, caught in the shoulder by a shot from one of the guys in the car.

There was the sound of a cheer from below.

Now the three soldiers wavered. A giant wolf was bearing down on them, but on the other hand, men with guns had just shot their friend. Who to aim at?

They froze when Peter stopped. He opened his jaws in a grin.

"WHOOOOOO'S FIIIIIIRSSSST?"

They screamed—every one of them—in sheer terror, and with a laugh, Peter took two bounds to one, ripping his throat out before he snapped his jaws around the leg of an escaping soldier and dragged him back. A swipe of his claws ended the man's screams.

The third one ran for the top of the other hill, the lookout point where the last two soldiers were. They were motioning him away, perhaps under the absurd idea that if he ran somewhere else, Peter wouldn't notice them. However, with him running at them, they also didn't dare shoot at Peter. The Bitches were going to have a good laugh about this when he got back.

Someone in the clearing below brought down the runner, and the last two soldiers panicked and tried to run. One of them caught himself in time, but the other stumbled and fell, realizing too late that there was nowhere to go. His scream pierced the air as he fell down the steep slope, and cut off abruptly. The other was dead a moment later, and Peter chuffed, wriggling his shoulder where it stung slightly. At least that one got a shot in. One out of eight wasn't bad, he supposed. Some elite fighting force that was.

He loped back down the hill, gathering the bodies and dragging them to the center of the clearing before transforming beside the car and putting his clothes back on.

"We get these bodies taken care of, and you all should be ready for extraction. Although there's a mystery truck out there somewhere."

"I know." Marcus crossed his arms and frowned at the van. "Is it at one of the buildings, do you think?"

"It could just be on a supply run or a break," William pointed out.

Peter nodded. "They probably didn't think there was any real reason to guard this clearing, so they half-assed it." He shrugged. "Too bad for them. If they'd had sixteen, they might have had a shot."

Marcus muttered, "Not against you."

Bobcat swore from the edge of the clearing.

The other three men turned to see him put his phone hastily back in his pocket.

"What is it?" Peter asked him.

"It's nothing. It's just, ah, I have to go back into town." He nodded at Peter. "You want a ride to the lab?"

"That'd be great."

"Right." Bobcat swung into the driver's seat. "I'll be back soon. You two, ah hide those bodies, and see what sort of fun toys they have in the truck."

"Where are you going?" Marcus asked him.

"I forgot a thing." And Bobcat backed out of the clearing at high speed, almost before Peter had time to close the door.

NATALIE GREY & MICHAEL ANDERLE

"Alright, bitches!" Tabitha kicked open the door to the server room and strode in, pistol pointed at kneecap height as she scanned the room. "Who wants to do the right thing and tell me what I want to know so I don't start shooting?"

"Weren't you going to start shooting anyway?" Hirotoshi muttered quietly.

"They don't have to know that." She looked back at the guys with a smile. "Come on, I'm perfectly harmless, there's no reason to look so scared."

"You're...ah...um..." One of the server room guards gulped when Tabitha looked at him. "You're holding a gun."

"And I won't use it unless you piss me off," she explained. "Come on, that's simple enough, right? You tell me what I need to know, and I don't have to kill everyone painfully." She smiled sweetly and arched her back.

Just a little.

Ryu and Hirotoshi exchanged a look. Painful death or not, every guard in this room was certain to die within minutes. They were here of their own free will and had not tried to escape or fight their employer. Information wasn't going to help them.

The guard who had spoken was emboldened by his exchange with Tabitha. "What do you need to know?"

"How many laboratories does Hugo Marcari have?"

All the guards looked away, suddenly evasive.

"Uh, no one knows." The guard forced a smile.

"Oh, dear. And it was such a simple deal we had, wasn't it?" Tabitha looked over her shoulder at Ryu and Hirotoshi. "I didn't make it complicated, did I?"

Ryu shook his head.

"I thought not." Tabitha sighed and shot the man in the

kneecap. "Ow. You're screaming very loudly, you know. Now, in the interests of your *other* kneecap, tell me about Hugo Marcari's laboratories."

"No one knows about all of them—it's the truth, I swear!" The man clamped his hand over his leg. His eyes were wide with pain and terror. "I swear!"

"Okay, so how many people would we have to speak to in order to find out about all of them?"

"I don't know!"

"Are you sure? Are you very sure?"

"Eight! There are eight!"

"Thank you." Tabitha shot him in the other kneecap and looked around at the shocked and horrified faces of the other guards. "Okay, new rule. If I have to ask a question more than once, you're going to regret it. Ah, ah, ah." Another shot rang out, and a man near the right wall collapsed with a scream. "Try to pull that alarm again and I'll kill you." She tilted her head to the side. "Do you know about any of the facilities?"

This man decided not to take any chances.

"Three. Velingrad, Sofia, and Istaravshan." He was panting, staring at her.

"Very good. Thank you." Tabitha gave him a beatific smile and looked at the rest of them. "Okay. Show of hands, who here knows of a facility that isn't one of those three?"

Seven hands went up.

"See, now you're all getting the hang of it. You first, with the mustache. Which do you know about?"

The man swallowed hard. Tabitha's gun was pointed right at him. "Naryn, in Kyrgyzstan. Naftalan—that's in

Azerbaijan. And Istaravshan, too."

"All right, we're up to five of eight. Who knows any other than those?"

A man raised his hand tentatively. "Khachmaz and Postojna. It's in the mountains outside of it. I think the eighth may be here."

"Think. Do you *know*?"

"I…" The man looked terrified. "I don't know. I didn't even know there were eight, I just wasn't sure if you knew about the one here and I—"

"Oh, shut up." Tabitha waved a hand. "Anyone else know of another location?"

Heads shook.

>>Those locations do line up with facilities we located from Gerard's phone. I suspected there was one more than he had visited, and this information has helped me locate that one as well. We have the information we need.<<

"Well, then. It was nice to meet all of you." Tabitha smiled. Behind her, she heard Hirotoshi and Ryu unsheathe their swords. "Now, I'm not sure how familiar you are with basic morality, but it is considered very, very immoral to stand by while a sociopath abducts families, tortures them, and forces them to kill one another."

"But—" one of the men spluttered.

"It was just a job!" another one insisted.

"Wrong answer." Tabitha shook her head at them and then considered. "Of course, there wasn't actually a right one. And now, if you'll excuse me, I have to be quick about this, as I'm in somewhat of a rush."

Gerard sat in a darkened conference room. He was alone. He had forbidden the guards from interrupting him. A few years ago, he had begun wondering what would happen if Hugo were ever to die suddenly—either violently, or simply by accident. It was not the sort of thing Gerard's father would ever have wondered. Hugo's father, Mateo, had married and had three sons in quick succession. His parents had sent two to boarding school while Hugo was raised as a pampered only child. There had always been a backup plan if Mateo died young. Hugo had not only never married, he arranged to have both of his brothers killed as soon as he took his father's place.

All of which led Gerard to wonder. He never spoke these thoughts aloud, and he rarely even admitted them to himself. It was considered treason to speak of the death of a king, and Hugo had considered himself a king. Therefore, Gerard never even broached the subject. He also knew that Hugo believed close servants and wives should die with their master. It wasn't a traditional Spanish custom, simply one that appealed to his pride.

Or rampant egotism, to be more accurate.

In fact, as Gerard wasn't certain that Hugo was dead, he was sure that he was expected to break down a door, escape from this facility, and battle his way past whatever was in the castle to get to Hugo's side. If he had failed to protect his master, he would be expected to commit suicide next to the body.

But if Hugo was not yet dead, he would be soon. Gerard had seen the way these enemies swept through the Velingrad facility. They had found Hugo here, at what should have been a protected location, within days. They would keep coming, and eventually, they were going to win. And when Hugo was dead, the empire he was building would collapse.

Which meant there would be nothing left for Gerard. Unless he took matters into his own hands. The question, of course, was whether he dared.

The sound of gunfire decided for him. Gerard stood up decisively, gathered the three flash drives that held all of the research, and slipped out of the room, running for the hidden staircase that was not on any of the blueprints. He wasn't planning to go down with the ship, and he wasn't about to throw himself on his sword just because a noble was dead.

He sneered.

Hugo's talk of nobles and commoners had been embarrassing. The truth was, nothing mattered but power. And when Gerard had that power, the world would bow at his feet just as it had been prepared to bow at Hugo's.

16

Catalonia, Spain

"ADAM says to go around to the back entrance." Nathan looked around the corner of a nearby building. "Apparently, the guards are optimally spread if attackers come in the main doors."

Irina grinned. "We'll catch them unawares."

"Not exactly," Nathan explained. "I said they were optimally spread for that, but these guys actually are well trained. They're ready to shift their positions and offer one another backup as soon as they know where we are. Which means—"

"Take them down quietly before they know we're there?" Stoyan suggested.

"Exactly."

The three of them eased around the corner and walked purposefully down the alleyway toward the back door.

>>**Nathan, I'm trying to keep the power out and keep control of the computer systems, but there were failsafes built in to disrupt an attack like this. I'm not sure**

how long I can hold the darkness or the auto-locks on the doors; I think some of them have already been breached. This building has better systems than the castle.<<

Nathan told ADAM. "We'll move quickly. Thank you for the warning." He explained to the others what ADAM had said, and added, "This means that the Wechselbalg might escape and not know who we are. Be ready."

"We are," Irina told him. "I remember that when the cages came open at Velingrad, we thought it might be a trap. We will move quickly, and hopefully, by the time they are brave enough to get out of the labs, they will see that we are killing the guards."

"Let's hope so," Nathan replied grimly. He reached out and eased the door open.

The back stairwell of the building was bathed in red light. Their footsteps echoed as they made their way quickly to the door into the building and paused to listen for movement outside.

>>They are around a corner from you.<< ADAM told Nathan. >>I think they are looking the other way, but my imagery is not exact enough to tell.<<

Nathan shed his clothes and transformed. He stood still, panting slightly, as Irina and Stoyan put on his armor. Stoyan also transformed, and Irina practically held her breath as she opened the door carefully and motioned the two wolves through. She followed, easing the door shut behind her, and transformed as well.

The wolves moved carefully and quietly through the halls. Even in human form, they had enhanced senses, but in wolf form, they could hear the quiet shifting of the soldiers around the corner from them. The men wore bulky armor and helmets, which meant that the sound of their own tiny movements and breath kept them from hearing the faint sound of the wolves.

Nathan looked around the corner first. The soldiers were watching double doors in the middle of the hallway, half pointed away from them and half pointing toward them.

With one paw, he motioned for Irina and Stoyan to stay where they were, and he looped around the other way and through a side passage. If they attacked from both sides, they would cut off the avenues of retreat and sow confusion. It looked like there were only about a dozen guards here, which meant that there were twenty-four unaccounted for. Nathan moved carefully through the halls, listening for noises and the hum of any electronics.

At the other end of the hallway, he took a moment to examine the six soldiers he planned to take down. The bulletproof vests were made to protect against human weapons. They had big gaps at the necks and arms, and their legs did not have plated armor.

There were a dozen ways he could kill someone wearing this armor, and it would hardly be difficult.

He crept around the side wall, chose his first target, and padded up silently behind him.

Whether the man felt Nathan's breath on his neck, or whether he had some sixth sense that a predator was behind him, he turned quickly.

Too quickly, and without a plan.

Nathan raked his claws across the man's throat. Blood

sprayed out over him and the man went down with a gurgle before he had the chance to scream.

It was enough sound that the men in front of him turned, but it was not gunfire or a yell—and the soldiers at the other end of the corridor did not realize anything was wrong until it was too late. They were still leaning forward, squinting into the dark—some fiddled with night-vision goggles—when Stoyan and Irina attacked.

Then the screaming started.

The next soldier in Nathan's sights had been peering at the fallen body of his friend. His eyes were looking at a human height, not at the height a wolf could crouch, and his confusion and panic grew when the screaming began. He looked over his shoulder sharply.

It was the last thing he did. Nathan leapt, teeth snapping across the man's throat as they skidded into a group of three soldiers behind a barricade.

They turned at the noise, but not fast enough.

Nathan's jaws snapped around a man's upper arm and he thrashed his head side to side, digging into the arteries as the motion snapped the man's neck. The second man stood up to kick him as if he were an unruly puppy.

He still hadn't realized just how big a Wechselbalg was. Nathan stood up on his hind legs, paws closing in and down on the man's shoulders and dragged him to the ground. The last thing he saw was gleaming eyes and a long snout, as Nathan's claws took him in the throat.

A bolt of pain shot across Nathan's back and he snarled. The third man had drawn his sidearm and fired. A moment later, a second shot from the last of the six men caught him in the other side.

There was a snarl and a scream as Irina took out the sixth. She pivoted and pushed off the floor, leaving the man's dead body behind her as she jumped at Nathan's fifth attacker. There was no reason to land softly, so she let the momentum carry her heavily down, crushing his chest even as her claws sank into the spaces between armor plates.

She yipped worriedly at Nathan.

He shook himself and gave a noise halfway between a growl and yip—it hurt, but he was all right.

They all heard the sound of the door opening the next minute, and loped around the corner.

A single figure stood there.

As they watched, Peter transformed and shook out his fur. He opened his jaws in a grin.

"HOOOOPE III DIDNNNN'T MISSSSS THE FUNNNNN."

When the power flickered off with a groan, Hsu felt her heart seize.

It was beginning.

She knew what she had to do, but it still took her a moment to force herself into motion. Below her, guards yelled commands.

They thought it was just a good opportunity to test their knowledge of the building in the dark. Hsu's mouth curved into a smile. They might not even live long enough to realize they'd been wrong.

She didn't care about them, though. She had a plan.

She strode out of her lab without looking back, even as the wolves whined and clawed at their cages.

She had plans for them, too.

She went to a small room at the end of the corridor. She had found it a few days before, and realized that Hugo, in his paranoia, had provided her the perfect tool—a cache of weapons, meant to be accessed by the guards in case the experiments broke out, and protected only by a padlock.

She couldn't see the numbers, and so she moved the dials one by one until she heard the faint click. In the darkness, she felt carefully for a pistol and a few spare magazines. She shoved them into her pockets, hoping that all the pistols and magazines went together, and made her way to yet another room—the backup power.

The scientists here were also paranoid, and they, too, had given Hsu the best gift she could imagine: a private way into the system of radio waves that controlled the Wechselbalg.

She reached up and hauled with all her might on the crank. It moved slowly with a terrible screech at first, and Hsu redoubled her efforts. She had to get it working before anyone found her here. She had to be able to start those signals.

It took mere minutes for the soldiers in the courtyard to realize they could neither batter their way out the front gates nor into the main castle. The building was old, eminently defensible from any brute force a human body could muster on its own. Its electrical system was faulty enough—having been wired into a structure that wasn't made for it—that ADAM's control of the computer system could not be thwarted.

But the castle had been made for sieges, and that meant that there were stairs running up to the walls, and into the castle itself. Soon, there were ten soldiers pounding up the steps and toward the shadow.

Which was when they saw Stephen.

And the wolf.

It was like something out a nightmare: a man in all black, with a young face but old, old eyes that gleamed blood red, and claws. A man drenched in blood. A man with no kindness in him at all, and no fear of the wolf that stood far, far taller than a wolf should be. There was blood on her fur and her teeth, and an unmistakable anticipation in her eyes.

The soldiers, to their credit, really did try.

They took shelter behind the outcroppings of stonework designed to slow the flow of enemy soldiers into the castle and fired with weapons that were loaded and ready.

But before they had even seen him move, Stephen was among them, landing softly with a flare of his coat. He smiled pleasantly.

"You should never have agreed to guard Hugo. You should have cared why he had so many enemies. He earned them. By standing between us and our duty, you have made us your enemies as well. This is your last chance to walk away."

The men wavered, looking at one another.

Stephen stood quietly. He hoped they would take his

offer. The bloodlust that was rising in him made him want to lash out, but he knew they didn't understand what had been done here, what atrocities had been committed. He had seen enough of the world, to hold himself in check while he waited for their response.

Jennifer's snarl alerted him. Stephen turned and ducked in one fluid movement as a bullet shot by overhead.

It should have hit him in the back.

He'd given them a chance to make a choice, and they had.

They really had.

Stephen's eyes glowed red as Jennifer leapt into the air. Her claws hooked into the fastenings of the man's armor and she dashed his body against the parapet, against the stone walkway, and against the barriers until he was limp, and her jaws were coated with blood. She looked up with a low growl and no one there needed any help understanding what it meant.

Hurt him, and I will make you pay.

To be shot in the back after offering parley was infuriating, but to watch the man you most loved in the world shot in the back after offering parley induced pure, unadulterated rage.

Jennifer wanted them dead, and she wanted them to know how badly they had misjudged before she killed them.

She watched as Stephen launched himself into the fight. He was a true warrior, poetry in motion, a marvel of simple, deadly movement.

Claws raked, and his fists moved fast enough to crush the men's chests with brute force.

They had bullets?

Bullets were nothing.

Stephen was one of the first of Michael's line, and he had been given new life by the Matriarch.

No armor, no weapons these men had could protect them from him. They raised their guns to fire and he was on them in a blur. They died choking on their own blood, as their necks snapped, or in a sudden wave of pain as their focus on Stephen blinded them to the threat of the wolf.

When it was over, Stephen stood, his claws coated in blood, his coat torn. He looked around at the faces of the men who had stayed true to money over honor.

And then he looked to Jennifer and handed her his coat.

She smiled at him as she slipped it on, and walked unconcerned through the field of bodies and toward the stairs.

"I wonder if there's any fun left to be had at the lab," she suggested.

"Quite possibly." Stephen smiled as he followed her down the steps. "They had three dozen of the new soldiers, not two. I say we take the trucks and make a grand entrance."

"I do like that idea." Jennifer smiled at him. "Just as long as no one tries to shoot you in the back again."

"Between people trying to shoot me in the back and earning your ire, and people trying to use you as an experiment and earning mine, I see this being a bad day for just about every one of them," Stephen joked. He handed over her weapons and swung up into the seat of one of the trucks. "Race you there?"

Hsu made her way down the hallways, quietly determined.

She was ready.

The idea had come to her in the middle of her first night here, with astonishing clarity. She knew what she had to do, she just had to hope that it would work.

The panel that controlled the commands was lit up, glowing strongly in the dark room. Hsu sat down at the desk and gave a look over her shoulder at the wolves. She could see the gleam of their eyes.

It occurred to her that, much like the last time, she might find herself at their mercy once again. Hopefully not.

She took a deep breath and typed the commands into the computer. It had taken her some time to find a way to do this. The system really wasn't set up for it. When she pressed the button, it was with a silent prayer.

There was a clang from behind her as the commands took hold.

Or, really, suggestions.

There are men here in all black, with guns. They are not your friends. But there are also those who are Wechselbalg, like your-selves. They have come to rescue you. Transform back into humans, open your cages, but stay in the labs until your allies come to tell you the hallways are safe.

She watched the power from the generator die until it barely had any strength left for the end of the message.

She looked toward the door in indecision. Should she risk trying this again?

The sound of footsteps decided for her. Hsu sank down

behind the desk so that no one passing by would see her, but tried to sneak a glance at the window.

Her heart stopped.

Gerard was walking past quickly, making for the back of the building.

She was glad she'd stopped to pick up the gun. Legs shaking, Hsu made her way to the door and followed him into the darkness.

17

Catalonia, Spain

The drive should have been pretty, through rolling hills filled with vineyards and gnarled olive trees. The dust on the road kicked up into a clear blue sky.

Maurice could enjoy none of it.

He spent the rest of the drive in a state of paranoid hyperawareness. Every car that approached him produced a spike of fear, and when they passed by without trying to run him off the road, he felt dizzy with the rush of relief.

The three drivers did not talk with one another. Maurice imagined the other two also white-knuckling their steering wheels. They just wanted to get through this.

He was so tired. The others must be, too, but no one suggested they stop. Maurice opened his window to let the winter air buffet him, waking him up with the chill, but it was already fading into a pleasant warmth.

They came to the town around midday.

The directions for the drop off had been very exact, but

he found himself doubting them. They weren't even on a proper road.

They kept driving, skirting the edge of the town and, at last, turned into a hollow clearing in the hills.

There were two men waiting. No car.

The back of Maurice's neck prickled. Something about this wasn't right. He almost shrank away as one of them approached his truck.

"*Bonjour.*" His French was perfectly accented, and he continued flawlessly. "Are you Maurice?"

"*Oui.*" Maurice stared at him. "I didn't know you would speak French."

"*Mais oui.*" The man flashed a smile. "You can unhook your trailer and continue into town."

He seemed so friendly that Maurice felt himself relax. More than anything, he wanted to stretch his legs and sleep. He didn't care about the order. But he also thought he should help this man. He opened the cab and climbed down.

"I can help you load the goods when your trucks come," he offered.

"That won't be necessary." The man's pleasant smile didn't waver. "But thank you. You didn't have any more trouble on the road after those cars, did you?"

Maurice stared at him, chilled again. "How did you know about that?"

The man's eyes slid away from his. He clearly wasn't prepared to answer that. "I am sorry," he offered. "We didn't think you would be a, er, target."

"Thank you for everything," the other man cut in. He gave the first one a sharp look. "I'll help you unhook your cab, and you can be on your way. The money should already be transferred to your employer's account."

Maurice swallowed. He nodded jerkily as the second man started unhooking the lines to the cab.

The five men worked in silence. Maurice's fellow drivers gave him sharp looks, clearly questioning what explanation he'd been given for everything, and Maurice could only shrug helplessly. These men seemed fairly nice. They hadn't demanded anything else before payment, and they hadn't even looked in the trucks.

They'd even seemed genuinely sorry about the armored cars.

How had they known about that, though?

Unless….

Unless they had been the ones who somehow ruined those cars and made them drive off the road.

Maurice redoubled his efforts. He was even more terrified now. If these men could do that, he wanted to be gone from here as soon as possible.

The three drivers climbed into their cabs with a quick farewell and drove away without another word. No questions. No jokes. You didn't ask questions of people that had clearly gotten a shipment of weapons, and you definitely didn't joke with them.

It was only when he was halfway back to the town that he noticed the missed calls on his phone—eleven of them, from Henri. With a muttered oath, Maurice dialed Henri's number. He was not surprised when Henri picked up at once.

"Tell me you're still driving," Henri answered immediately.

"No. We left the trucks."

Henri swore inventively.

"What? What happened?" Maurice felt anger start. "Did they not pay?"

"Oh, they paid," Henri assured him. "But we had another offer. The same amount, to delay as much as possible and stay with the trucks. The offer was from the Chinese government, if you can believe it. Can you go back?"

Maurice shook his head before remembering that Henri couldn't see him. He chose his words carefully. "Henri, we were attacked on the road, and the attacks were stopped—by something… These people have powerful enemies. They are powerful, too. It is best to take the money we have, and not get in the middle of their fights. You don't want to be a witness to any more of this. I say we liquidate the company and take new names. Make it difficult for them to find us later. I don't know what this was, but it must have been bad."

He had never contradicted Henri like this, and he could tell that the man was surprised.

But finally Henri replied, "I understand. Whatever was in those trucks, it is best if we never know more about it."

Maurice nodded as he hung up.

It would be a long time before he stopped looking over his shoulder, he decided. It would also be a long time before he stopped wondering what had been in those trucks. Drugs? Weapons? There was no way to know.

He could only go to church, beg forgiveness, and then try to start over.

He was lucky he had escaped with his life.

William scrambled up to the top of the shipping container and opened a small window to peer into the darkness.

The radio at his side crackled. "How do they look?"

Bethany Anne. He suppressed a smile.

"Everything looks all right from here. They're in the boxes, and the boxes are wrapped to keep out moisture."

"Tracking devices?"

"I'm sure of it," William answered without hesitation. "But we have a few things up our sleeves that they aren't expecting. As soon as Bobcat's back, we'll be able to get all of this taken up immediately."

It was risky to have the Pods come down in the middle of the day, but after the attacks on the road and the "accident" with the blown tire in the Pyrenees, they'd decided that it was best to extract the shoes while Hugo's newly hired soldiers were busy fighting off Stephen and the rest.

Bethany Anne gave a small sigh that transferred through the radio in a tiny puff of crackling. "And we still don't know why they were trying to destroy the shoes?" She sounded one part contemplative, one part mortally offended that anyone would even think of destroying designer shoes like that.

"Not the faintest idea," William admitted. "We thought they wanted to track them."

A shout came from below. Marcus waved up at him and cupped his hands to shout. "Sixteen tracking devices so far!"

William shook his head as he climbed down from the

shipping container. "I really don't get it, then. Maybe they just wanted to piss you off, ma'am?"

"Well, they've succeeded." Her voice changed. "Wait. Why are you waiting for Bobcat? Why isn't he with you?"

"He said he had to get something in town," William explained. "I'll tell him that the trucks are here."

"Do that," Bethany Anne advised. "Tell him we don't have time to fuck around on this one. As soon as you've disabled those tracking devices, the shoes need to come up. ADAM just intercepted a transmission from the Chinese. They're trying to hire mercenaries. I'd get out of there soon if I were you."

William swore. "Thanks. I'll get our devices up and working, and I'll tell Bobcat to get back here. I don't even know what the hell was so important that he had to go back."

Bobcat's phone rang, and he fumbled to pick it up while keeping his eyes on the road. He was coming into town now, and in this sleepy little town, the road was dotted with chickens, goats, and people ambling to and fro.

He honked and swerved.

"What is it?"

"The shoes are here," William told him. "And we have to leave soon because the Chinese—get this—are calling in mercenaries."

Bobcat rolled his eyes as he swerved again and took a corner too hard. He waved a hand at an old lady who shouted after him in Catalan.

"You need to come back," William insisted urgently. "Right now."

"I'll be there as soon as I can."

Bobcat hung up before William could say anything more. His phone started to ring again, but he didn't answer it.

The warehouse was only three streets away. The warehouse...and his seven crates of rare hops. His supplier had refused to leave the warehouse to bring him the crates early, so Bobcat had to retrieve them himself.

Except that, as he came around the corner, he realized *why* the supplier had said they couldn't leave just now.

Seven trucks of hired guards had come into town the night before. Two had gone to the castle. Three had gone to the laboratories. One had gone to the drop point.

And one was here.

Waiting. In the town.

Bobcat took a hard left and swerved around the back way, picking up speed. He heard a shout behind him and swore. With one hand, he dialed the number of his contact here.

"*Si?*"

"Open the warehouse back doors," Bobcat shouted into the phone. "And be ready to close them immediately!"

It occurred to him, vaguely, that most people would have turned around and made a run for it.

But most people, in his opinion, didn't care nearly enough about *beer*.

Peter transformed as he loped up the corridor, and he opened the door into one of the labs cautiously. His eyes swept the room and stopped at the prone figure of a scientist, a tall man whose head had been crushed in an animal's jaws.

He could not see the Wechselbalg.

But he could hear them, faintly. They were waiting to see who he was.

"I am one of you." Peter gestured to his naked body then transformed quickly.

They came out at once and he transformed back.

"We were told you were coming," one of them offered in Spanish. "Are the hired guards dead?"

"Not all of them," Peter admitted. "But we have two trucks coming to take you to safety, and there is a safe path to the outside." He paused. "Who told you we were coming?"

"One of the scientists. They told us through the machine." The woman pointed to the switchboard. "Could you not hear it?"

"The labs are shielded from the outside," another one explained to her. "If you aren't in the room, you don't feel the signal."

"I thought you needed a chip to feel the signal." Peter was worried now.

"No. It can be done to anyone." The woman shook her head. "It isn't safe in these rooms. We need to get all the prisoners out as fast as we can."

Peter nodded decisively. "We'll move quickly. Go to the right when you get out, take those stairs, and exit out the back stairwell. Two people will arrive in armored trucks. We'll handle any fighting."

The Wechselbalg hesitated.

"There was another facility like this in Sofia," Peter told them quietly. "In Bulgaria. They decided to stay and fight, because they wanted the scientists and guards to suffer. All of them were killed. We don't want that to happen here. We will make sure that these people pay for their crimes, but we want all of you to escape as well."

The Wechselbalg nodded. They had seen proof that Peter was one of them, and they understood the necessity of getting their children out. They might regret not striking the killing blow themselves, but they knew that it would fall.

"Thank you," one of them murmured, as they took their children and joined the stream of Wechselbalg in the halls, following Irina to the back exit of the facility.

They were moving quietly, but Peter knew it was only a matter of time until the rest of the guards found them. In the darkness, he picked out Nathan's form as he started ascending to the next level, using the stairs at the other end of the hallway.

Peter nodded to Stoyan to follow him to the other set of stairs.

He could smell the coppery scent of blood in the air. The Wechselbalg had already taken their vengeance on the scientists.

Now it was up to the Queen's followers to take care of the guards.

Jennifer parked the truck outside the back doorway and left it running as she moved to open the doors into the interior. Stephen parked beside her and left his truck running as well. He moved quickly and efficiently as he prepared the inside of the truck to hold as many escapees as possible.

Jennifer smiled. It seemed especially satisfying to be using the guard's equipment to help the Wechselbalg who were trapped here.

She looked around when the back door opened slowly and Irina poked her head out. The woman smiled when she saw Stephen and Jennifer, and motioned some people out into the alleyway.

They moved quickly, blushing at their nakedness, and Jennifer made sure to meet their eyes and smile as they piled into the truck. One or two of them recognized her, and one man told her, "I am glad they didn't figure out what you were."

"They did in the end," Jennifer replied. "Well, Hugo did. But I took care of him."

There was a ragged cheer from the group of escapees.

They kept streaming through the doors, and soon both trucks were packed.

Jennifer handed the keys to one of the men, who was dressed in a thin, ragged shirt and pants. "Here. There's a map on the front seat, and I marked it with where to go and leave people. There should be three trucks and three guys there. I'll call ahead to let them know that the people in the armored trucks *aren't* the guards."

The man laughed. "Thanks. I'd hate to get shot at by allies. I'll come back with the truck to get the next set, too."

"You don't need to worry," Jennifer explained. "There are three more trucks here. We can take those."

They waved as the trucks drove away, and waited for Stephen to bring the other trucks. His coat was enough to make Jennifer look normal while she drove, but she would definitely turn some heads if she tried to walk around the building and to the parking lot in just that.

When the rest of the Wechselbalg were loaded into the trucks, Jennifer gave them directions and they drove away, toward freedom.

>>**Marcus and William have been informed that these trucks are holding allies.**<< ADAM told her. >>**We will begin extraction at once.**<<

"Thank you, ADAM. And, where's Bobcat?"

>>**Bobcat is in a warehouse. I cannot trace its ownership and neither Marcus nor William seems to know what he's doing there. He claims it's important.**<<

"Well, there's only one thing that's important to Bobcat, you know." Jennifer grinned. "Beer."

>>**Most interesting. I had not considered that.**<<

"I wasn't serious. Bobcat wouldn't risk his neck for beer."

>>**Are you sure?**<<

"...No."

Gerard was three floors up when he heard the door open, and footsteps beginning to climb the stairs behind him.

They'd sent an assassin, had they? He backed into the

shadows to wait, when his footsteps stopped, so did those of his pursuer.

There was a pause, while they tested each other's resolve.

Then the pursuer's footsteps resumed.

Gerard's lip curled. Fool.

He waited until they were halfway up the flight below him then stepped into view, with his gun pointed.

He stopped. The Chinese scientist? He felt a rush of satisfaction.

"The truth, if you please." He kept his voice light and controlled. He knew she would give some tedious speech about ethics and helpless animals, but he wanted to know what her plan had been. He wanted to hear her say that he had been right.

He only wished Hugo were alive to realize that Gerard had been right all along.

But he was wrong about her. She didn't give a tedious speech. Her face hardened, her arms rose, and there was the crack-boom of two shots.

She'd seized her best opportunity, but it wasn't enough. Gerard had already been aiming for her, and all he had to do was squeeze the trigger. Hsu hit the wall with a cry of pain and slid down it, leaving a smear of blood as red spread across the shoulder of her white lab coat.

18

The bullet had torn the skin on his calf.

Gerard waited, blood soaking into his pant leg and dripped down his leg. The pain was surprisingly hot, as if the bitch had prodded him with a hot poker instead of shooting him.

And he still didn't have her answer. He was never going to hear her say that he had been right about her. He hated that almost more than he hated the pain.

His hand trembled on the gun. He wanted to empty the rest of the bullets into her out of sheer spite, but he might need them. He'd heard the fight on the first floor.

They would keep coming, these people. They were not going to rest until they had won.

Or until they *thought* they had won.

He smiled slightly.

His satisfaction did not make him sloppy, however. His gaze did not waver, and he did not move. He waited while the stain spread slightly across the scientist's lab coat, waited until she did not move and did not cry.

Then he turned and took the stairs as fast as he dared. He had to get to the roof.

She wouldn't be the only one coming for him today. He was sure of it.

So much pain. Heat spread through her until it almost became a chilling cold, and pain followed in its wake.

Shot. No coming back from that.

As Gerard's footsteps receded, Hsu fell to one side, gritting her teeth against a cry. She was not going to scream. She was *not* going to give herself away.

Pushing herself up took everything she had, and she realized she'd left the gun on the ground. Her right shoulder was a mess, and the fingers wouldn't close around it. She grabbed it awkwardly with her left and dropped it into her pocket.

She knew she should apply pressure to her shoulder, but she needed her left arm to hold the railing and haul herself up the stairs. She didn't look back at the bloody fingerprints, and she didn't look up at the number of stairs she had yet to climb.

Wherever Gerard went, he would hurt people.

She wouldn't let him leave. All that mattered was ending this.

Bobcat practically bounced with impatience while he watched the crates being brought out onto the warehouse floor. Each crate of hops was carried carefully, wafting the fresh scent across the room. His supplier, Resi, checked each crate carefully for damage then lifted the lid to peer inside. They were weighed, painstakingly.

Under his breath, he murmured, "Hurry it up!"

This was taking forever, and he didn't have forever.

Although he wasn't using his time well, either. He should be using this delay to come up with a good enough excuse that Marcus and William wouldn't want to look in the crates. And a good enough excuse to put the crates somewhere they couldn't smell them.

So far, he hadn't come up with anything.

Bobcat. Bethany Anne's voice.

Uh-oh.

"Yes?" he managed. He hoped his voice didn't squeak.

What the hell is taking so long? Marcus and William say the trucks are there, the trucks with the Wechselbalg are on their way, and you aren't returning their messages. Is this the fourth grade?

"No, no. No. Of course not." Bobcat managed a laugh. "I'll be back. I just needed to get a...thing. Equipment. Thing."

What sort of equipment thing?

"Uh..."

Let me be very clear. Bethany Anne's voice was sweet. *If I lose even one pair of my shoes because you were off doing God-knows-what, I am going to make you sorry you were ever born. I am going to make you clean the entire asteroid with a toothbrush, and I am going to make you do it while wearing the most uncomfortable pair of heels I own, and then I am going to make you replace those heels once your big feet have stretched them out. And then, if I do not feel you are appropriately contrite, I am going to make you paint every single one of your helicopters pink. Are we clear?*

"You wouldn't—"

Am. I. Clear?

"Yes, ma'am." Bobcat hurried over to Resi. "You know what? Five crates are good. I'll be leaving right fucking now."

She frowned at him. "You're going to have to wait anyway."

Bobcat felt his heart sink, "Wait for what?"

With an impatient sigh, she turned the video monitors toward him.

Bobcat dropped his face into his hands. Outside, on the street, was a barricade. The last twelve soldiers had taken up position, weapons aimed at the doors of the warehouse.

Resi shrugged. "We've got a long wait, friend. Unless you think you have some way to get out of here without them noticing."

Bobcat frowned, an irritation in his voice. "Well, that's not exactly my style..."

Jason Velley knelt on the street and waited impatiently, his grip tightening around the stock of his gun.

The street was entirely silent. The residents had complained, but in the end, they allowed themselves to be evacuated into the nearby town center. The name "Hugo Marcari" seemed to be magic around here.

The soldiers had all thought it was going very

smoothly. Of course, that was until everything came to a halt. There wasn't any shouting or clanking from inside the warehouse, and their tech support back at HQ couldn't figure out what the warehouse was for in the first place.

They kept claiming it was for beer supplies.

Jason rolled his eyes. Under the layers of body armor, sweat started to drip down his back. His knee ached against the cobblestones, and it wouldn't be too long before his back started to cramp. He wasn't a sniper, for God's sake, just a normal hired guard, and what he had thought was going to be a fun shootout—the sort of adrenaline high he lived for—was turning out to be a lot of waiting.

He was a professional, though. He remained motionless, and waited for the warehouse doors to swing open. As soon as they did, the people inside would see that they were surrounded.

Jason smiled to himself. The successful capture of arms traffickers was going to look very good for his firm—and for him.

He was sure he would get a raise by the end of the summer.

They were on the third floor when they caught up with the bulk of the new forces.

Most of the scientists had apparently fled this way as well.

>>I see forty-eight heat signatures on this floor.<< ADAM informed Jennifer. >>It appears that all twenty-

four of the remaining new guards are here, as well as fourteen scientists and ten of the old security force.<<

Stephen asked, "What about Gerard?"

>>I am not able to tell if Gerard is on this floor. I can see a difference between guards and scientists because of the amount of metal and electronics they carry, but I have not identified individual heat signatures.<< There was a pause. >>There are two figures in the back stairwell. One is ascending faster than the other.<<

Stephen and Jennifer exchanged a look. They didn't need to talk in order to understand the other one's thoughts. Neither of them had any intention of letting Gerard slip away—and if someone was weaseling out of the fight, it was almost certainly him.

They nodded to one another.

Jennifer turned to Nathan and the other Wechselbalg. "As soon as we reach the stairwell, Stephen and I will split off and follow Gerard to the roof. The rest of you..." she smiled.

Stephen also smiled, coldly. "Can judge those who are here," he finished. "There may be those, like Hsu, who have been captured and forced into work—and who have dedicated their efforts to ruining the research efforts. But if any should stand between you and your duty, you will do what is needed."

"And even those who were captured may not be worthy of survival," Irina added quietly. She looked at Nathan and Peter, and her chin trembled slightly. "I saw those who should have fought, who were also captives and should have been on my side, work for Hugo instead. They started to enjoy hurting us. Hsu was one of the only ones who tried to work against Hugo. I don't know if there will be any here, beyond her, who should be spared."

"Do not worry," Nathan told her gravely. "My Queen has been accused of many things, most of them lies—but being too lenient on dishonorable people isn't one of those things."

Peter laughed softly.

The Wechselbalg transformed, and Stephen opened the door to let them slip through.

The corridors were eerie and silent. Red emergency lights gleamed at regular intervals, but in between, doorways and alcoves lay in shadow.

Jennifer's nose twitched as she used all of her senses to determine what was ahead. ADAM would not always be there to give her a layout of the battlefield, and, in any case, she was accustomed to figuring it out herself.

After their performance in the castle, she didn't think much of these guards.

There were several ahead and to the left. She could not quite hear their breathing or smell their fear sharply, so they must be some ways along the corridor.

With Peter at her side, she padded to the corner and peered around.

There was a shout, and bullets ricocheted harmlessly off the wall. Jennifer and Peter chuffed at one another. The shots hadn't even been close.

"Let me handle one or two of them," Stephen suggested from behind them. He waited for them to dip their heads, and then snuck a peek. He laughed as well when the second burst of gunfire was no more accurate than the first. "Idiots," he muttered.

Then he moved, a blur in the darkened corridor. There were screams, and the deeper noise of a pistol shot.

Jennifer did not wait for an invitation. She came around the corner and broke into a run. One of the gunmen looked over his shoulder and his eyes widened.

He was swinging around to face her when she jumped and had only turned halfway when she pushed off him and leapt again, over Stephen's head where he was fighting. She landed hard, already turning, and her jaws clamped around the leg of one of his opponents.

He went down with a scream.

Then Peter and Nathan were in the fray, Stoyan and Irina joined them scant seconds later.

Stephen moved in a blur as he ran for the door to the stairwell. "Jennifer! This way!"

She stood on her hind legs to take down a man who had aimed at Stephen's receding form and stepped daintily over his body to follow her boyfriend.

Stephen was laughing at her when she arrived. "You're so delicate about *stepping* in blood, but you've got it all down your jaws."

Shrugging was difficult as a wolf. Jennifer lifted her muzzle and practically pranced past him into the stairwell, accompanied by the sound of his laughter.

"Right," Stephen agreed when he'd managed to catch his breath. "Let's go fuck Gerard up, shall we?"

There was a clatter from inside the warehouse, and the sudden revving of an engine.

Jason gripped his gun and exchanged a quick look with the rest of the men.

It was finally starting.

His eyes narrowed as he looked at the door.

"Come on," he muttered. The second those doors started to swing open, he was going to start firing.

Except they never did. With the sound of splintering wood and a revving engine, the antique car they'd seen earlier came crashing out of the warehouse, fishtailed, and accelerated down the street as the guards stared after it, mouths hung open.

Jason recovered first.

"To the truck!"

Shit, shit, shit. They could not lose this guy. He gestured urgently for the men to pile into the back of the armored truck.

"What was he yelling?" Sean demanded.

Jason hesitated. He couldn't possibly have heard it right, could he?

Because it really sounded like the driver had been shouting, "FOR BEEEEEEEEEEER!"

19

Catalonia, Spain

Dust and gravel shot out from under the wheels as Bobcat pushed the GTO to the limits of the big 389ci's engine. Ordinarily, it would have been an ideal day to take an old car on country roads and see what he could make it do, but the gunfire made it a little less fun.

No, actually, the gunfire made it more fun.

Except for the part where the bullets might ruin some of his cargo. He shuddered at the idea of hot bullets burning the precious hops and jammed his foot down as hard as he could on the accelerator.

A scatter of gunfire hit the road to his left and he slouched to make sure his head was entirely behind the headrest. He'd outfitted this car with every kind of toy he could think of—even missile launchers—but they wouldn't help if he wasn't behind the soldiers.

He swerved as he led the truck down the road. As an armored vehicle, it wasn't made for pursuit—which was

NATALIE GREY & MICHAEL ANDERLE

good, because no matter how gorgeous it was, the Pontiac couldn't possibly compete with one of today's sports cars.

A round of shots came far too close, one hit the other seat's headrest and sent a shudder through the car. Bobcat kept swerving, trying to keep his movements as erratic as possible. They were almost out of the town now, but—

Were those police lights behind them?

Oh, shit.

He pressed the phone to his ear., "Come on, come on, come on. Pick *up*."

"You're finally on your way back, huh?"

"Marcus!" The wind tore his voice away. "Yeah. I have company."

Marcus swore. The captive Wechselbalg had just arrived and were waiting for their Pods, and none of them were exactly dressed for combat—nor did he want them transforming and taking the chance of getting hurt. Not now. Not when they were so close to getting away entirely.

"Get back in the trucks!" he yelled to the crowd. At least they could shelter there for a while.

He thought furiously and came to a conclusion. "Bobcat?"

"What? I'll be there in a few."

"No, don't!"

"Don't?" Bobcat practically screamed the word into the phone. "I am in a '65 Pontiac GTO and I am being followed by an armored truck! I am being shot at!"

"Yeah, see if you can lead them off for a while." Marcus could see the two puffs of dust approaching. "I'll tell you when it's safe to come back. I'm going to call in extraction."

Bobcat sputtered, "Did your mother make it with...with...."

"Yes?"

"A box of rocks!"

"No," Marcus informed him seriously. "Or if she did, I don't want to know about it. Thanks for helping out."

He hung up the phone on Bobcat's yells of protest and called up to the *ArchAngel*.

QBS *ArchAngel*

The call button on Phillips's desk buzzed.

"Phillips."

"Slight change of plans." The computer identified the voice as Marcus. "Can you get those Pods down to us ASAP? I'm thinking five for the evacuees and the three with the shielding for the shipping containers. And one for us, with shielding for the car."

The team had developed an airtight shield that would snap closed around a suspended shipping container, keeping the delicate glue and leather safe during the ascent into space. A few tests in some remote areas of Canada had shown that the process worked well.

They had wanted to do this at night, so no one would notice the Pods, but that plan had been abandoned as soon as the mission got moved up. They had also not wanted to do this during a shootout, but it looked like they weren't going to get that wish, either.

Phillips would normally have raised her eyebrows at a request like this and told the ground team to stick to the plan, but she had been informed that any request from the ground team was likely to be made because things had gone sideways.

Apparently, that wasn't uncommon when dealing with the types of enemies TQB had.

"Stand by, ground team, Pods will arrive very shortly." She tapped another button to put herself through to the infirmary. "Doctors to the landing bay, please. We are expecting numerous passengers with unidentified injuries, some may be serious."

She turned back to track the Pods' progress through the atmosphere. Even after having seen another mission, she could still hardly believe how quickly the Pods moved. Even free fall through the atmosphere was nowhere near as fast.

They were approaching the drop point.

Despite herself, she held her breath. She could try to assist and respond as quickly as humanly possible, but when it got to this point, she could only watch and pray.

Catalonia, Spain

Bobcat caught the sight of the descending Pods out of his peripheral vision and took a sudden, sharp left onto another road.

He couldn't let the driver of the truck see those Pods. So far, he didn't think they'd figured out that Bobcat was leading them in circles, but that illusion wouldn't hold for very long if they saw alien technology coming to hover over a nearby hill.

"'Try to draw them off,'" he muttered, mocking Marcus's voice. Was the man insane? Did he think Bobcat was happy to just drive around with a target practically painted on his back?

The truck honked. He looked over his shoulder and saw that they were motioning for him to slow down.

They were clearly frustrated that they were getting nowhere, and he was almost tempted to see what they had to say.

Except, what were the odds that they would just shoot him?

The truck swerved and put on a burst of speed, jolting dangerously over bumpy ground beside the dirt road, and the driver leaned out the window to yell.

"You should surrender!" he called in English.

Bobcat snorted.

In reality, he wasn't pleased to realize that the only thing keeping the truck from coming up alongside him was that they were afraid of driving off-road. This wasn't good for him.

"We've called in backup!" the driver yelled. He pointed to the curve of the hills. "We have another truck there—just surrender now, and we won't hurt you!"

While they might make that claim, they inevitably planned to turn him over to Hugo, who definitely would hurt him.

Which made this guy a liar.

A damned liar.

"No thanks!" Bobcat called over.

"Just surrender!" The driver was clearly frustrated. "You know you're going to have to sooner or later!"

Except he'd seen those Pods coming down, and he was

NATALIE GREY & MICHAEL ANDERLE

pretty sure he'd just seen one go back *up* in his rearview mirror.

"ADAM? Is the castle clear?"

>>Yes. All of our personnel are out, and the building was entirely cleared before they left.<<

"And could you, ah, could you arrange for some sort of poison or something to take out these guys as soon as they arrive?"

>>Lethal or non-lethal?<<

"Lethal. They've had their chance to back down, and they just lied to try to get me to surrender to Hugo."

>>Noted. I can take care of it.<<

"Thank you." Bobcat looked at the truck and grinned at the driver. "Tell you what," he shouted. "I'll race you back to the castle. You know, so you can see the wolves."

The driver went white as a sheet. "Wolves?"

"Yeah! Wolves! Hugo's been breeding these really big wolves." Like hell he was going to admit what they actually were.

"There are actually wolves?"

"Sure!" Bobcat spun the wheel and nearly jolted his teeth out of his head with a bumpy ride back to the road. "Come on! You should definitely see them!"

There were shouts as the truck accelerated back toward the castle, leaving him in the dust.

Bobcat laughed until his sides hurt. Then he wiped his eyes, turned the car, and headed for the drop point.

———

"This way." Marcus held a child's hand so they could climb

up into the darkness of the Pod. The first was already away and the other four were loading quickly.

"Where are we going?" the child asked him. His dark brown hair lay in soft waves against his head. Behind the bruises and the too-thin frame, and beyond the instinctive fear he had learned in the labs, he had the curiosity of any child. He wanted to be going someplace good, even though he'd stopped believing that would really happen.

Somehow, that hope made the rest of it even more heartbreaking.

Marcus tried not to clench his hand around the boy's fingers. He wanted to leave, go to the lab, throttle the scientists with his bare hands.

How dare they do any of this?

Instead, he forced a smile. "You're going to a ship," he explained seriously. "It's called the *ArchAngel*. There are people there who will make sure the people who hurt you can never hurt anyone else. Ever again."

The kid gave a trembling smile.

Behind him, a woman laid her hand on his thin shoulder. She had the same eyes as his, large and dark, and she'd wrapped a blanket over her naked form. She ushered him into the darkness but stopped to look at Marcus.

"Why are you helping us?" she asked him.

"Because it's the right thing to do," Marcus told her simply. "Someone who hurts people like that? They have to be stopped. Don't worry—where you're going, you'll be safe. I promise. And Hugo is going to die."

The woman smiled then. "I know. I met the people who were going to kill him. Thank you." She pushed her way into the darkness.

"All Pods are loaded." The communications officer on the ArchAngel spoke quietly in Marcus's ear. "Should I begin extraction?"

"One moment." Marcus gave one last look at the interior of the Pod and gave a thumbs-up. Once they all gave thumbs-up back, he retreated to let the door snap closed. He checked the other three as well. "All right, we're good. Take 'em away."

"Stand by."

The Pods rose into the air with astonishing rapidity, and Marcus stumbled forward in the rush of air they left behind.

William was just hopping down from the last storage container. He tapped his ear. "Take 'em up fifteen feet."

The Pods rose into the air and hauled the storage containers along with them, creaking slightly in the wind. Devices gleamed at regular intervals along the sides. They were blocking the tracking signals embedded in the containers.

"Sec…." William pressed a button on a control pad.

The sealant systems snapped closed around each one of the shipping containers, and the control pad blinked green.

"Ha!" William gave Marcus a high five. "Take 'em up! Let's get those shoes in orbit!"

The containers shot skyward, following the Pods full of escaped Wechselbalg, and the two shaded their eyes to watch them disappear from view.

They turned at the sound of a car. A few seconds later, Bobcat's GTO pulled into view and screeched to a stop. Bullet holes and dents pockmarked its sides, and everything in it—including Bobcat, himself—was coated in dust.

"What the hell happened to you?" William asked.

"Marcus decided I should be the bait in a car chase," Bobcat explained. He gave Marcus a look. "Something for which I have not yet forgiven him."

"You enjoyed it," Marcus shot back, grinning. "Bet you had fun yelling insults at them." He frowned. "Speaking of which, where are they?"

"Oh, they're on their way to the castle. I think they'd heard there might be wolves, so when I mentioned wolves—"

"You told them about the—"

"Let me finish. As I was saying, when I told them about the wolves at the castle, they went racing off. They won't find anything," Bobcat added. "But ADAM will have a nice surprise waiting for them when they get there."

"Nice as in…" Marcus raised an eyebrow.

"As in, lethal." Bobcat gave them a look. "They tried to get me to surrender to Hugo, the bastards. 'We won't hurt you.' Yeah, sure, you'll just turn me over to a mass-murderer who runs torture labs. Don't ask me to feel sorry for them." He waved a hand as William went to pick up one of the boxes. "No! No. I'll get those."

"Why?" William asked suspiciously.

"Just because. No real reason. You, ah…you hook up the car. And don't look in the crates. They're filled with…spiders…"

Marcus and William gave the crates a side-eye, but they hurried to hook the car up for its shielding.

"This thing's beaten up enough that it's going to take forever to restore," William muttered.

"Yeah, but how could you not?" Marcus questioned. He

patted the flank of the car affectionately. "It's a car with *rocket launchers.*"

"Yeah, I see your point."

A few moments later, they heard Bethany Anne's voice in their earpieces.

"Is everything good to go? Because it looks like your friends in the truck might have realized they made a mistake, and those police cars followed the truck at first, but now they're calling in backup to where you are."

"Shit!" Bobcat hurried to load the last crate into the Pod. "Come on, guys! Move! And someone figured out how to take out an armored truck!"

"We'll handle that with some pucks," Bethany Anne informed them. *"You all get your asses out of there. And Bobcat, get ready for an explanation as to why you went into town and got an armored car chasing you in the first place."*

Bobcat swallowed. "Yes, ma'am."

They hurried into the darkened interior and everyone leaned back in their seats as the door snapped closed and the Pod began to ascend.

In the darkness, Bobcat heard two noses sniff at the faint, herbal scent wafting out of the crates.

"Bobcat," Marcus began conversationally.

"Yeah?"

"You know you're going to have to share those hops with us."

Bobcat sank his head into his hands as Marcus and William started laughing.

Back to square one.

20

Catalonia, Spain

His leg was aching fiercely.

Gerard swore as he limped around the roof, readying his escape. A video monitor near the door showed a view of the town, quiet and quaint.

And the pile of explosives in the village square.

The people of the town didn't know what they were, but his pursuers would—and this would buy Gerard his escape.

For far too long, he'd lived in a world that held back the strong and lifted up the weak. It was why he had been glad to serve Hugo, initially. One could only restrain the natural order for so long. It was best that the strong were allowed to rise and establish themselves.

But he had been held back, as well, by Hugo's antiquated ideas of honor.

There were only two kinds of people in the world—the strong and the weak. The weak had no other purpose but to be pawns in the games played by the strong.

Hugo had always rambled on about the duty of lords to their serfs. True, he demanded their service—and at times, their lives—but he believed it his obligation to provide them with peace and prosperity.

Gerard had no such ridiculous ideas.

He would create the world he wanted. For *him*, not for some outdated notion of chivalry.

This was why Hugo was dead, and Gerard was alive. He would fly away from here, safe, while the scientists bled out downstairs. None of them had been strong enough to win on their own.

He paused. Except, of course, Hsu.

He admitted to himself, grudgingly, that he could at least admire her somewhat. After all, she was the only one who'd had the courage and the brains to persist in her goal.

The rotors on the helicopter shuddered into motion, and Gerard smiled. Where Hugo delegated everything to pilots and secretaries and administrators, Gerard would do everything himself. Now that he thought of it, it really was incredible that it had taken this long for Hugo to be assassinated. The man had been a complete idiot.

Gerard shook his head and checked the fuel and pressure gauges one last time.

He didn't even hear the shot. He just felt the blinding pain as he tumbled sideways out of the helicopter and hit the concrete. His arm was on fire, and there was a ringing in his ears. He turned his head slowly and saw a mess of blood.

He'd left his gun on the seat of the helicopter.

He pushed himself up woozily and turned.

"You?"

"You were pointing the gun right at me and you didn't think to shoot it again?" She spoke Bulgarian with a sneer, making him translate rather than deigning to speak his mother tongue. "Idiot. You deserve to die for that alone."

Her finger tightened on the trigger.

He threw his hands out. "Wait!"

"Do you really think anything you say now will sway me?"

"Yes." He began to laugh. The sound was too high; he really was losing a lot of blood. "There are bombs in the town. If I'm not still alive in twenty-five minutes to give a command to the computers, they'll go off. Do you know how many people live there?"

Her hand tightened on the gun, but she swallowed. "You're lying."

"Look at the monitor." He pointed.

She waited a moment, looking at him like she was sure it was a trap.

It was, but it wasn't a lie. The trap was her own honor.

"It's up to you," Gerard suggested conversationally. "Do you want eight thousand lives on your conscience or do you just want to let me go?"

"You'll set them off anyway."

"You know I won't. How does that benefit me?"

"How does it benefit you if you're dead?" she snapped.

"If I'm dead, I don't give a damn if the whole world burns," he told her flatly. He tried not to sway into the side of the helicopter. He was losing blood, but she was worse off. "What's it going to be, Hsu? Me and them? Or is everyone going to survive?"

She hesitated, and that was enough. He took two quick

NATALIE GREY & MICHAEL ANDERLE

steps and grabbed his gun, and she dove out of sight behind the monitor as he shot. Her answering shot was wide and he hauled himself into the helicopter, laughing.

He threw his head back with a feral grin as the blades picked up speed and the craft rose into the air.

There were only two types of people. And underneath all of that resolve, Hsu was weak.

That was why she would always lose.

He set the course into his computer and reached over for the med kit.

Now he just had to make it to the airstrip, and then to the facility, before the blood loss got him.

On the roof, Hsu hung her head. Tears splashed, hot, over her hands.

She'd missed her shot. There was no way she would ever forgive herself for this.

The door behind her burst open and a man ran out onto the roof, followed by a wolf. The man swore as he watched the helicopter recede.

"Not. Again." He forced the words out through gritted teeth.

Hsu tried to push herself up and found her legs were too weak. She fell, blue sky above her.

"Are you all right?" The man's face swam into view. Handsome and young, it would have been flawless if it hadn't also been spattered with blood.

"He said...bombs." Hsu felt her face screw up and she let out a sob. She hadn't wanted to go out like this, crying like a baby, but she had failed at the one thing she swore she would do to clear her honor.

One thing.

"What?" The man said something rapidly over his shoulder. His lips moved, but she couldn't hear him, and he bent close. "Who said what? Gerard?"

Hsu nodded. She didn't see the point in saying anything else, but he really seemed to want to know. "He said there were bombs in the—oh, God, it hurts—in the town."

She could have sworn she saw something plummeting out of the atmosphere toward her, a tiny speck of black that was growing larger…

She closed her eyes. "He said he had to be alive in twenty-five minutes or the bombs would go off and everyone would die and I…I fell for it." Her voice trailed off in a sob.

The man lifted his head, almost as if he were listening to something she couldn't hear. Then he looked down at her again.

"There *are* bombs," he agreed gravely. "I've just had it confirmed."

"How—"

"No time. We need to get you medical care."

Something whistled nearby and hit the ground with an audible shake. Hsu looked over to see a black metal orb. It snapped open and spat something out onto the ground: a bag, which the wolf picked up delicately in its teeth and brought back. It nosed Hsu, a strangely comforting gesture.

"You remember Dr. Yordan?" the man asked as he rummaged in the bag.

Hsu's eyes went wide. *"You're….* You were a shifter? The whole time?"

The wolf sat down. It was grinning. It seemed very pleased with itself.

"Dr. Yordan—actually, her name is Jennifer—is the reason we were able to find the facilities," the man told her conversationally. He took out some scissors and began to cut the cloth away from Hsu's shoulder.

"Shouldn't we—Gerard—the bombs—"

"Ah. That's being handled. We have one more thing to do, but first, you need to be stabilized. Now, I'm afraid this is going to hurt." He grimaced at her, and then his fingers darted, faster than humanly possible, into her shoulder.

She screamed, and he held up a bullet with an apologetic wince.

"Don't worry, we'll make that shoulder as good as new. Now, what's your blood type?"

"O-negative."

"Ah, the rarest of the rare." He rummaged in the bag and pulled out a container of blood, which he hooked up to her. A moment later, a cool bandage settled over the wound on the front of her shoulder, and he levered her up carefully to lay another bandage against the back. He smiled at her. "It's going to itch horribly, but it will heal. I promise. No infection, no scars, no nothing."

Hsu stared at him, trying to decide if this was a dream of some sort. Blood loss, probably. Was she dying? Was she actually here, on the roof, or was she still in the stairwell, just dreaming about taking her revenge?

The man looked her quizzically. "Are you all right?"

"Trying to decide if this is real."

"Ah. Quite real, I assure you. Now, if you'll excuse me for just a moment."

Stephen stepped away, nodding to Jennifer where she sat guard.

She made a little puffing sound. She would watch the scientist to make sure the blood was being absorbed properly and the bandages working. She settled down on the cool concrete and nosed at the scientist when she tried to push herself up. A tiny growl and a shake of her head told the woman to stay put.

Stephen walked a short distance away to speak to ADAM. He knew he should be angry. In fact, he *had* experienced a moment of pure visceral rage as Gerard flew away. The last thing he'd wanted was to be a minute too late again.

But not only was Jennifer not on this helicopter, he'd had the perfect idea.

"ADAM, would I be correct in assuming that you can send messages to any and all of the facilities?"

>>Yes.<< ADAM sounded curious. >>**What would you like me to say?**<<

"Explain to them that, after deliberations, this experiment has been deemed to be a failure. They will all receive raises and glowing recommendations, but should start the process of dismantling the labs and wait for trained personnel to come pick up the Wechselbalg."

>>**And then you won't have to fight at all. That's very smart.**<<

"Coming from you, I'll take that as a massive compliment." Stephen grinned. "And I suppose it goes without saying that this message should be from Hugo, right?"

>>I assumed as much.<<

"Just one more thing, ADAM. Put in there that Gerard unfortunately had to be fired but has taken a helicopter and may arrive at any of the facilities. It is my—Hugo's—wish that he be apprehended, and that they should not hesitate to use force if necessary. Even deadly force."

>>I admit that I am somewhat surprised you do not wish to take revenge on him yourself.<<

"I would like to," Stephen admitted. "He's a sociopath, and he has caused a great deal of suffering. However, one of the things I learned in my years is to arrange my world so that I don't need to do everything myself."

>>I see.<<

"Which isn't to say that I was perfect," Stephen hastened to add. "As you will know, when Bethany Anne found me, I had retreated from the world in defeat, thinking I could control nothing. I was wrong. But there is still much to be said for delegating, even if others don't know you've done so."

>>That seems a very practical outlook on life. One moment while I send this message. Sent. All administrators should receive it within minutes, and I will continue to track Gerard's helicopter. By the way, the bomb containment units have arrived.<<

"Containment units?" Stephen walked over to look at the monitors. Black casings now surrounded each of the bombs, and were rolling slightly over the not-quite-flat cobblestone streets.

>>It's the same material as Pods. It should contain any blast, though we will have to come up with a story to explain it. Due to the time sensitivity, there was no

way to avoid people seeing them land. Someone should go pick them up.<<

"I'll do it. And we'll need a Pod for the rest of the team. We'll want to make sure we're all cleaned up and re-armed before we head to whichever facility Gerard lands."

21

It was pouring rain as the helicopter touched down and Gerard looked around the deserted roof.

The administrator should be here to welcome him. Yes, the weather was forbidding, but that was no excuse.

Nevertheless, the lights glowed warmly inside the stairwell that led to the rest of the building.

With a scowl, Gerard stopped the rotors and disembarked.

He didn't run. If anyone was watching—as they should be, given that he'd sent advance notice that he was coming —they would not see him run frantically through the rain.

He tried not to limp, as well, but that was difficult. He'd managed to have an EMT brought to the helicopter, a man who widened his eyes at the bullet wounds but patched them up ably enough. Still, the more Gerard sat, the more his leg and arm both ached.

He made a promise to himself as he walked through the pouring rain and hauled open the door—if that scientist somehow survived, he would make sure to hurt her exactly how she had hurt him. He wouldn't be surprised to meet her again. She seemed to weasel out of every trap set in her way.

All in good time.

He made his way down the steps and was already one floor down when a door slammed open and steps hurried toward him.

The administrator, finally! Gerard stopped and raised an eyebrow so that the man could see he wasn't amused by this delay.

When the man came around the corner, though, Gerard could hardly conceal his surprise.

Most of the scientists he'd met were pale and painfully uneasy in their own skin. They looked like the sort you could knock over with a single punch. This man, however, was tall and broad-shouldered, with a nose that looked like it had been broken at least once, and watchful eyes.

And he didn't look at all frightened of Gerard.

"Are you the administrator?" Gerard asked warily.

"I am." The man studied him. "And you are Gerard Cordova, yes?"

"Yes," Gerard replied shortly. He went to push his way past the administrator.

The man's arm moved out to stop him, his hand closing around the injured arm with surprising strength.

Gerard shuddered with pain, and for a second, the man looked at him carefully.

"We have received word from Hugo about you."

For a moment there was real fear.

Had Hugo survived? If so, he would never tolerate

Gerard's desertion. There would be a price on Gerard's head, and he would die in agony as Hugo watched...

Then he remembered the truth. Even if Hugo lived, he could never win against Gerard.

Not now that Gerard had decided to make his move.

Gerard smiled at the man. "And what have you heard?"

"That you had to be let go, and have apparently not taken the news well."

Gerard did not let his smile waver, though his mind raced. That didn't sound like Hugo. Hugo would have said something about honor and loyalty. Which meant...

Those clever bastards. It was TQB, it had to be.

He could play the game, too. He smiled regretfully. "I'm not sure we should speak here. The truth is...well, let me explain."

He thought the man might object, but a moment later, he stood back, instead, to let Gerard lead the way.

They walked to the fourth-floor offices in silence. Once or twice Gerard caught the coppery scent of his own blood and hoped that the administrator did not smell it as well. He was oddly uncomfortable having the man at his back. Gerard was rarely physically intimidated by anyone, but this man had an air about him that said he could handle himself in a fight.

Gerard did not want him to see any weakness.

In the administrator's office, he made a point of taking the chair behind the desk. He pressed his fingers together as he looked up at the man's face.

"So, Doctor...."

"Elasov," the man supplied.

"Doctor Elasov. I was afraid that you might receive

Hugo's message before I arrived." Gerard shook his head regretfully. "You see, Hugo has not been well. You can understand, I am sure, that we did not want to say anything about this until now. We were hoping he would recover. However, it appears that will not happen, and thus, that we must take matters into our own hands to bring these experiments to their rightful conclusion."

"Hugo said the experiments were to be shut down." The administrator's face did not even flicker.

"I'm afraid he was incorrect. Well, I am sure he believed what he said. But as you and I both know, these experiments must continue." Gerard smiled. He wanted the man to warm to him, to be on his side.

It was not usually something he cared about, but he did not like the man's flat-faced appraisal of him.

"So much technology lies just outside our grasp," Gerard explained. "Why, if we but increase our efforts, we could—"

He broke off as the door swung open and the scientists came in.

Every one of them looked like as much of an athlete as the administrator, and indeed, most of them had shoulders that strained at their lab coats. They looked at Gerard curiously.

Gerard looked at the administrator, raising his eyebrows in a silent question.

"They should hear this as well," the administrator told him with a shrug.

Those were not his decisions to make, but Gerard would let that slide for now.

"Very well. To catch all of you up, there has been an

unfortunate incident with Mr. Marcari. He is unwell, and has begun turning on those who were once closest to him. While we are sure that he will recover someday, for now, we must continue his work without him."

There was a stony silence. The scientists staring at him were no friendlier than the administrator.

Gerard's nose twitched. The smell of blood seemed to have gotten stronger. He cast a quick glance at his arm and shook his head. No blood was seeping through the bandages at all.

He was imagining it.

"What I wish, more than anything, is that when Hugo recovers, he will find this program complete." Gerard tried to smile. He stood, brushing the desk with his fingertips, and kept the smile on his face as he looked over the line of expressionless faces.

What was wrong with these people?

"And, of course..." He tried to ignore the prickling sensation that something was wrong. "The best way to do that is to redouble our efforts. I would like to have each one of you select your most advanced subject for a demonstration tonight. We will begin immediately."

Silence. Not one of them answered.

"I will go change," Gerard announced, "and then we will begin." He was starting to be genuinely angry. They were hardly convincing him of their loyalty to the project.

He strode to the side door that led to the administrator's personal apartments and yanked it open.

And almost retched on the floor.

The bodies lay all across the room, blood pooled beneath them. The faces were shocked, wide-eyed, panicked—and utterly still. Claw marks raked across their chests.

Gerard felt his chest constrict. The blood he'd smelled...

The sound of ripping cloth caught his attention and he turned quickly, stumbling on his bad leg.

The people who had filled the room were not the scientists. They were wolves, advancing on him with their teeth bared.

"No! NOOOO!"

But they were on him a second later, snarling and ripping as they tore him limb from limb, and the last things Gerard saw were yellow eyes and bloodstained teeth.

One of them changed back, wiping the back of his hand across his mouth and laughing. He looked into the room where the rest of the scientists and guards lay dead, then down at Hugo's emissary.

Finally! After the days and weeks and *months* in this godforsaken place, they had relaxed. And the Wechselbalg had taken their revenge.

He spread his hands and turned, smiling. "Brothers and sisters, we have done it. We have killed the emissary. We will kill Hugo, too."

The wolves yipped in agreement. They were panting with the excitement of the hunt.

"When everyone who participated in this is dead, we will not stop there." The man shook his head, a smile on his lips. "No. We will not stop until the humans who allowed this to happen know the error of their ways. We will not stop until humanity itself realizes that *we* are the true masters of this world. Until *they* are the ones who slink in the shadows and we are the ones who rule. We will not stop until the world is *ours!*"

He threw back his head and yelled his fury as the wolves howled in agreement.

The world would pay for their pain.

EPILOGUE

"I'm confused. Don't we have to, you know, save the world?" Jennifer gave Stephen a grin.

He shot a look over his shoulder as he led her through the halls of the *ArchAngel*. "Sure. In the morning."

Jennifer laughed.

Her laughter trailed off when Stephen opened the door to their room. It was lined with candles and chrysanthemums, her favorite flower. A full bathtub, piled high with bubbles, stood in the corner, and a mouthwatering dinner was laid out for them.

"This is…" She looked at him. "Did you really come up with all of this on your own?"

"I did." Stephen picked up a glass of wine and handed it to her with an artful bow. "Not just a handsome face, you know."

Jennifer smiled as she drew him close. "That dinner looks amazing, but maybe a bath first."

"Should I go?" Stephen asked courteously.

NATALIE GREY & MICHAEL ANDERLE

"You are so old-fashioned." She kicked the door shut and grinned at him. "You're not going anywhere."

Safely returned to the *Meredith Reynolds,* Bobcat walked through the hallways, casting frequent glances over his shoulder.

Bethany Anne was going to absolutely ream him out sometime soon. She'd said something about giving him time to "make up a good story," but he knew he'd be on the receiving end of every ounce of her creativity when she gave him hell later.

For now, though…

He slipped into his private rooms and gave a sigh when he saw her.

Her. Absolute perfection.

"You're even more beautiful than I remember," he whispered. He walked forward to kneel in front of her, gazing up adoringly. Her scent surrounded him. "You're absolutely perfect."

The vat of beer bubbled, releasing its heady scent into the air as Bobcat laid his cheek against the copper.

FINIS

Thank you so much for reading Book 2 of *Trials & Tribulations*! When Michael and I first started talking, he asked about my favorite characters in the series and Stephen had already emerged as an early favorite. Getting to write about Stephen and Jennifer has been incredible!

As some of you know, I've also had a pretty cool milestone recently: the release of the first book in my new SHADOWS OF MAGIC universe. BOUND SORCERY was an amazing project, and I am already working on Book 2!

I hope you'll check out Nicky's story – there's magic, snarky druids, kickass heroines, punch-in-the-face-worthy villains (who get smacked down, don't worry!), and just a *dash* of romance. Happy reading!

As always, a huge thank you to the beta readers, the entire team, and most of all to Michael for allowing me to write in the Kurtherian Gambit world!

Sincerely, Nat

If you would like to join my mailing list, here is the link (and thank you!)

https://landing.mailerlite.com/webforms/landing/w0k9j4

Thanks to Liza Meyer and Keith Verret for the final WTF Where is the book? Posts ;-)

Here we go, the second book in *Trials and Tribulations* and can I say THANK YOU that not only did you read the book, but you are reading these *Author Notes*, as well?

I have to admit something. Fifteen minutes ago, I was editing *Awakened* by Ell Leigh Clarke and me when I happened to update a fan on Facebook with the latest Timeline to all things Kurtherian (It is here, if you would like to see it: http://www.kurtherianbooks.com/timeline.)

While I was updating the request for the timeline, I happened to see the post where I was talking about THIS book coming out.

OH MY GOD, I FORGOT! I had been waiting for a final cover from Jeff Brown for this book (we went from concept (what I showed everyone on Facebook) to concept 2, concept 3 and to me receiving the final finished cover about an hour ago.

I saw the final come through, but my laptop was having problems so it didn't refresh my content, and I didn't "see" the final image. It was just a lined box with nothing inside. However, by clicking on his name in Slack, it dropped the highlight to let me know he had something new and there is no reminder when you do that.

Then, I forgot he sent it until the Facebook comment of saying "I'm refreshing!" and my blood went cold.

Oh holy crap, I forgot! I jumped up and ran (ok, I'm almost fifty, I walked quickly) into the kitchen to pull this together and get the book up on Amazon and notify everyone on Facebook we are waiting on THEM.

Not me.

At least, I hope it isn't me.

Now, Jeff gave me the image only one hour ago as I write this, so it isn't like I'm too late, but I'm ashamed I even let it slip forty-five minutes like this.

Plus, I didn't have the *Author Notes* done!

Man, I seriously dropped this ball.

I hope you enjoyed *Damned To Hell* and I want to THANK the JIT team that helped catch a few last-minute screw-ups by the authors as we changed some locations and then boofed it up. We had a few discussions on whether Peter / Nathan / Stephen would act the way they did (and did some re-writes and discussions internally about guys, their motivations when their protective instincts rise up) and generally, loved Bethany Anne focusing on her shoes ;-)

Tonight, I go see *Guardians of the Galaxy 2* at 10:20PM. Until then, I'll be posting this book to Amazon, editing a scene in book 02 of the *Ascension Myth* series and editing book 01 of the *Ascension Myth* series titled *Awakened*.

I hope you have a great week!

Michael

From my Facebook Post when Natalie Released her first book.

Natalie Grey is a ghostwriter. In our business it (usually) means that she writes books, and NO one knows she ever did it. The author working with her to put it out (they are collaborations usually) hires her to write most of it and then they will edit and place their own name on the book.

I reached out to Natalie months and months ago and offered her the same deal that Craig, Justin etc. have. However, for her family, she couldn't jump on the deal since her family NEEDED the income the ghostwriting brings in.

Money up front trumps long-term income when it means food on the table, am I right?

However, I refused to treat Natalie anything but as an equal partner, who was just paid differently.

So, we created a unique Pen Name for Natalie, one that would work to give her a foundation so that if she wanted to try her hand at her own books, she absolutely could because her association with TKG would give her a name.

A name she could hang her writing hat on.

Now, the first Natalie Grey (solo) book is out and I couldn't be more proud that she has done this and I wish her the MOST success for her personal series. (We are about to drop book #03 that we have done together, so more Natalie Grey is coming!)

If you are interested in what she has done, here is the US Amazon Link to her book. If you are in another country, try searching on the ASIN which is B072BJYNZ8 .

My Book

Shadows of Magic

Bound Sorcery

Blood Sorcery

Bright Sorcery

Set in the Kurtherian Gambit Universe

Bellatrix

Challenges

Risk Be Damned

Damned to Hell

The Lost Years

The Vigilante Chronicles

Vigilante (1) Sentinel (2)

Writing as Moira Katson

Shadowborn

Shadowforged

Shadow's End

Daughter of Ashes

Mahalia

BOOKS BY MICHAEL ANDERLE

For a complete list of books by Michael Anderle, please visit

www.lmbpn.com/ma-books/

All LMBPN Audiobooks are Available at Audible.com and
iTunes. For a complete list of audiobooks visit:

www.lmbpn.com/audible

CONNECT WITH THE AUTHORS

Natalie Grey Social

Email List

https://landing.mailerlite.com/webforms/landing/w0k9j4

Follow Natalie on Amazon

https://www.amazon.com/Natalie-Grey/e/B01MYG7K8P/

Facebook

https://www.facebook.com/Natalie-Grey-393234677682987/

Michael Anderle Social

Website:
http://kurtherianbooks.com/

Email List:
http://kurtherianbooks.com/email-list/

Facebook Here:
https://www.facebook.com/TheKurtherianGambitBooks/